Golden Stranger

DIAMOND
SPIRIT

ALSO IN THE
DIAMOND SPIRIT SERIES
BY KAREN WOOD:

Diamond Spirit

Moonstone Promise

Opal Dreaming

Brumby Mountain

4
DIAMOND
SPIRIT

Golden Stranger

KAREN WOOD

ALLEN&UNWIN
SYDNEY · MELBOURNE · AUCKLAND · LONDON

Allen & Unwin
83 Alexander Street
Crows Nest NSW 2065
Australia
Phone: (61 2) 8425 0100
Fax: (61 2) 9906 2218
Email: info@allenandunwin.com
Web: www.allenandunwin.com

Cataloguing-in-Publication details are available from the
National Library of Australia www.trove.nla.gov.au

ISBN 978 1 74237 858 9

Cover photo by John P. Kelly / Getty Images
Cover and text design by Ruth Grüner
Set in 11.3 pt Apollo MT by Ruth Grüner
This Book was printed in March 2014 at McPherson's Printing Group
76 Nelson St, Maryborough, Victoria 3465, Australia.
www.mcphersonsprinting.com.au

3 5 7 9 10 8 6 4 2

For my little wildies,
Annabelle and Ruby

1

SHARA WILSON PEEKED through her dorm window curtains across the schoolyard. Soft rain fell, grey and drizzly, onto the asphalt, blurring the light and muting the usual morning bird calls. In a nearby building, plates clattered and cutlery jangled as kitchen staff prepared breakfast. A vacuum cleaner hummed down the hallway.

She glanced at her laptop, sitting among a mess of textbooks, notepads and pens on the tiny desk next to her bed. No one had warned her how much homework Canningdale College dished out. It was all she ever seemed to do. One more sleep, though, and her parents would be here to pick her up. Shara would be taking Rocko, her big brown quarter horse, home for three weeks of riding and hanging out by the Coachwood River with her friends.

Shara grabbed a popper juice and some biscuits from her drawer and took her laptop from the desk. She flipped it open and sat cross-legged on the bed watching it come to life. Back home in Coachwood Crossing, she knew her bestie would be doing the same. She logged in to chat and within seconds there was a pop-up message from Jess.

> Sharsy, check out this link! There's going to be a WILD
> HORSE RACE at the Coachwood Crossing Show.
> They're using real brumbies! Can you believe it?

Shara groaned. Jess would be in a huge tizz about this. She and her boyfriend Luke had been crazy about brumbies ever since Luke brought a herd of them back from Mount Isa last summer. Shara got comfy on the bed and clicked the link.

It took her to the program for the Coachwood Crossing Show, which started the next weekend and ran for three days. She scanned the list of events – it looked more like a rodeo this year, with campdrafting, calf roping, bronc riding and barrel racing. Then she spotted the wild horse race billed as 'Lunchtime Entertainment'.

This exciting event will use real mountain brumbies, wild and untamed!

Shara screwed up her face. Roping down wild horses and traumatising them just for the fun of it: how wild and exciting. Not. She typed with one hand, her juice box in the other.

> **Totally cruel.**
> I wrote to the show society and asked them not to hold the event and they didn't even answer me.

A bell clanged, signalling breakfast was ready.

'Are you coming?' asked Shara's roommate, Stacey, emerging from the small bathroom with a freshly made-up face.

'Nah, I'm good.' Shara held up her juice. She got back to her chat with Jess while Stacey pulled on some shoes and slipped out the door.

> **Why all the rodeo events this year? Are they still doing the cowpat lotto?**

That event had been Shara's favourite. The committee marked out the entire arena into squares and everyone bought a number. Old Harry Blake would release one of his cows onto the field and every time she lifted her tail, there'd be a roar from the crowd. The winning number won the loot. Harry used to supply stock for the mini campdraft and the potty calf ride, too.

No, since Harry died they've been using new stock
contractors. Some new mob from NSW are doing it.
All the events have changed.
Damn. I won fifty bucks once!

Shara got up and went to the small bathroom that she
shared with her three roommates, stopping quickly in
front of the mirror to tidy her straw-blonde hair into a
ponytail and splash some water onto her face. When she
got back, she found a tirade on her laptop screen.

The new contractors are so dodgy! They buy brumbies
that have been trapped in the national parks. Poor
things, one day they're free and the next they're on a
transport truck. It must be terrifying for them.
I can't believe they can do that.
We need to make a bold anti-cruelty statement,
Sharsy.
A what?

As Shara read the long-winded reply, she realised Jess
was in earnest, and had already recruited Rosie and Grace
Arnold.

Are you serious?
They have to be stopped. Brumbies deserve to be

4

protected, not roped and thrown in front of a crowd
of idiots. Look at this!

A YouTube video link flashed before her. Shara clicked
it, and a commentator's voice boomed *'Go!'* A dozen or so
cowboys ran across an arena, wrenched open the chutes
and released eight totally freaked-out brumbies. Before
the horses had taken two leaps forward, they were yanked
off their feet by teams of men, pulling them by the head
and forcibly restraining them.

Shara felt sick as she watched the desperate struggles
of the brumbies. Some broke free, others bolted with men
hanging off their necks or being dragged along on their
bellies on the end of a rope. Some horses were thrown
to the ground and had their ears bitten by the cowboys,
while others escaped but then galloped through the ropes
of other horses and got tangled. It was mayhem. Shara
was also struck by how unskilled the men were.

**I've seen people catch brumbies without needing to do
that. Why are they making such a mess of it? Losers.**

It was true. Skilled horsemen could catch brumbies in a
matter of minutes in ways that were gentle and quick.
This event was total crap. These horses were intentionally
mishandled just to give the crowd a laugh.

Are you in, Sharsy?

Shara hit the keyboard without hesitating.

Yep.

She asked Jess to email her with the details and logged off so she could get dressed – riding jeans, collared T-shirt and boots. She was still stuffing her shirt into her jeans as she emerged from her room and wandered past the dining hall on her way to the stables and Rocko. The bacon smelled great, but there would be plenty of that when she got home to Coachwood Crossing.

It always seemed to take forever to get home: five hours of driving along winding roads and long smooth highways with Shara's dad's baroque operas tinkling out of the stereo; through the hustle of Brisbane and up the Bruce Highway towards Coachwood Crossing. They turned onto a small tarred road with potholes that the council never fixed, and followed the bends and curves of the Coachwood River. Barry slowed the car as they crossed the railway line and rolled into town.

'Welcome home!' he said.

There were more cars than usual in the main street, and Shara noticed four men in big black hats and dirty jeans, standing outside the bakery eating pastries. The town was coming alive for the annual show, and she felt a rush of excitement. They'd be getting more than they bargained for this year!

As Barry drove past the derelict service station, the showgrounds behind it came into view, already bustling with people. A ferris wheel had been erected and tents were being put up. Miles of flagged bunting marked out the car park, and a few livestock trucks had already arrived.

Two kilometres on, they swung into their long, steep concrete driveway which ran down past a huge quadruple-bay shed and into a large gravelled yard cut into the hillside. Hex, Shara's shaggy yellow bitser, gambolled out to greet her, followed by Petunia, her little foxy cross.

Not much had changed since she'd last been home. Her older brother's Holden wrecks, a haven for mice and snakes, still sat in a row along the fence with grass growing around them. David had finally given up on them two years ago and headed north in a Mazda to work on prawn trawlers.

Near the house, a feed and tack shed sat just inside the horse paddock, which was lush with native grasses. The rest of the property sloped down in rolling hills and ridges grazed by purebred Droughtmaster cattle, her father's hobby.

Shara had barely led Rocko from the float into the horse paddock when Hex and Petunia went nuts, alerting her to a posse of three riders cantering beside the shady creek at the bottom of the property. Shara waved madly and did star jumps. *'Coo-ee!'*

Jess, Rosie and Grace let themselves through the bottom gate, then thundered up the steep hillside, squealing and laughing and scattering Barry's cows. Shara glanced nervously at her dad, who looked mildly annoyed but tolerant. 'Sorry, Baz,' she grinned.

He muttered something and wandered to the house.

Her friends' horses were blowing heavily when they halted in the yard. Jess, small and nimble, squealed as she took a dramatic leap from Dodger's back and landed with her arms around Shara's neck.

Shara laughed and squeezed her. 'So good to be home!'

2

THE NEXT MORNING, Shara scanned the yard to check that no one was about. She unzipped her jacket, pulled out two cans of coloured hairspray and stuffed them into Rocko's saddlebags.

She felt a queasy twist of nerves in her gut. At school, five hundred kilometres away, this had sounded like a fun idea. But now that the day had arrived, she was beginning to think she must have been nuts to let Jess talk her into it. Were they actually going to go and sabotage a rodeo event in front of the entire town? She'd never done anything so *out there* in all her life!

Shara swallowed hard, breathed in and ignored Rocko's usual cranky face as she hoisted herself into the saddle. Too late now – she was committed.

As she rode past the house she could hear the ever-present sound of the washing machine swish-swashing its way through the mountain of dirty clothes she had brought back from boarding school. 'I'm going now, Mum,' she called in through the back door.

'Okay,' her mother sang from inside. 'Have fun!'

'Oh, I think I will,' muttered Shara.

Hex and Petunia pulled at their chains as she rode past, wanting to come for the ride. 'You'll have to stay behind today, my stinky ones.'

Home disappeared behind her as she turned off onto an adjacent trail. Before long she heard a trotting horse approaching, and Jess appeared around a bend on Dodger. Jess held her reins at the end of the buckle and let the old bay stockhorse pick his own way over the rocky track. She pulled Dodger to a stop when she reached Shara, green eyes sparkling with mischief. 'Got your spray-paint ready?'

'I can't *believe* you talked me into this,' said Shara.

Jess laughed. 'I can't believe you *let* me talk you into it.' She turned Dodger towards the Arnolds' place. 'It'll be great. Come on, let's get Rosie and Grace.'

At the Arnolds' gate, Rocko raised his head and neighed loudly. Rosie, immaculate as always, trotted up on Buster. 'This is insane. Those rodeo guys will make dog mince out of us.'

'Only if they catch us,' said Grace, riding up behind on a dishevelled grey. Unlike her sister, everything about

Grace was a mess. Her jeans had holes in them and her helmet had stickers peeling off. It was always hard to believe the two were even related. 'But I don't intend to get caught.'

'My *parents* would make dog mince out of *me*,' said Shara. 'Getting caught is not an option, okay, guys?'

The girls rode down a steep easement onto the flats and cantered through a series of river crossings. As they neared town, they slowed the horses to a walk and rode single-file along the edge of the road before splashing into the creek that ran around the perimeter of the showgrounds. The show was clearly in full swing, with the ferris wheel rolling and carnival music twanging through the smells of popcorn and hot dogs.

'Did you talk to Elliot about getting photos, Grace?' asked Shara, ducking under a low-hanging branch.

'Yep, he's all ready,' said Grace. 'He's going to get a front-row seat so he can take photos and then send them straight to the newspaper.' She pulled her buzzing phone from her pocket. 'Oh, here's a text from him now. He says the brumbies have been moved to the yards behind the secretary's tent.' She began thumbing a message back.

'I know where that is!' said Shara, turning Rocko up the bank.

'Oi!' called Jess. 'We don't want to be conspicuous. Let's just tether the horses here.'

'Mmmm, smell the Dagwood dogs,' said Shara, inhaling deeply as she tied Rocko by the river.

'They're making me wanna puke,' said Jess, who was a fresh-food freak. 'Those things should be illegal.'

Shara and her friends emerged from the creek bed and hurried alongside a tall cyclone-wire fence that ran along the perimeter of the competitors' area. As they walked they peered through the wire mesh at the cluster of trucks and floats.

Horses were tied everywhere. Some people stood talking in small groups while others polished saddles. A cowboy practised roping on a straw bale with a set of horns attached to it. Ramps strewn with horse rugs and open bags of rodeo gear sloped to the ground from the backs of big horse rigs, in which rows of saddles and bales of hay were stacked.

'Look!' Grace pointed excitedly. 'Is that them?' On the other side of the fence was a huge red semitrailer with a double-deck stock crate on the back. On its cabin door were swirly gold letters:

Bred to Buck
Conneman Brothers
Rodeo Stock Contractors

'That's them,' hissed Jess. 'They're the new stock contractors, trading on the misery and trauma of wild horses.'

'Harry would never have let this happen,' said Rosie. 'This new show committee has no idea.'

The girls continued on foot until they came to the abandoned service station. Behind a rusty gas tank was a hole in the fence, through which local kids had been sneaking into the showgrounds for decades. The girls slipped through one by one and came out at the back of a brick toilet block. They squeezed along the narrow gap and walked out unnoticed into the backstage competitors' area.

They made a beeline for the secretary's tent, passing the stockyards and the contractors' semitrailer. Three scruffy, bony horses stood tied to its side. A small, taffy-coloured mare whinnied anxiously over the din of carnival music. Her dull red coat was thick and rough, and her creamy tail hung to the ground in matted coils.

'Reckon she's a brumby?' asked Shara, noticing the thickness of her bones and the slight feathering at the back of her fetlocks.

'Probably,' said Jess. 'Wonder why she's calling?'

'Maybe she has a foal somewhere,' said Grace. 'That's how our brood mares sound when we wean the foals.'

The mare screamed again and a man appeared from

behind the tailgate carrying a stockwhip. He was lean-jawed and leathery, with a half-smoked cigarette in his mouth and a freshly rolled one behind his ear. He swirled his whip and gave the horse a sharp crack under the tail. *'Stand up, feral!'*

The mare stood hard up against the truck, trembling, her head high and ears flattened. The other two horses jostled nervously. The man yanked the mare's rope so short that she could hardly move, re-tied it and disappeared.

Shara spun around to face Jess, her mouth wide open.

'Told you those Connemans were horrible,' said Jess. 'Wait till they get the brumbies in the ring!'

'Come on,' said Shara. 'Let's show them what we think of their wild horse race!'

When they reached the back of the arena they climbed up onto the rails and looked out over the entire show. In the distance were the pavilions and trade stalls, rides and jumping castles. People swarmed between them carrying showbags and fairy-floss sticks.

Directly under their noses were the rodeo pens. In a runway between the yards and the chutes, calves stood in single file, waiting to be roped. In the box next to the chute, Corey Duggin, Elliot's older brother, sat loose and supple in the saddle with the reins gathered in one hand and a lariat in the other. He was wearing a dark blue shirt, a classic black Stetson with a pinched crown, and faded denim jeans. Sampson, the sleek red horse he rode, shifted in anticipation.

Shara climbed right up onto the top rail, swung her legs over and lifted her chin to get a good view. Corey would be chasing points for the breakaway-roping national finals in a couple of weeks' time. This would be *fast*.

She watched as he ran a soothing hand down his horse's neck and sat calm and quiet, waiting for him to be still. Then he tilted his head towards the stewards and gave a small nod. There was a clunk of gates, and no sooner had a small steer bolted from the chute than Corey was after it, lasso whirling. He gave three quick swings of the rope and released it into the air, looping it over the horns of the steer. Sampson ground to a stop and as the steer reached the end of the rope, the loosely tied end broke away from his saddle, sending a small flag into the air, which signalled the end of his run and a blazingly fast time score.

'Woohoo!' Shara yelled. She turned to her friends and beamed. 'How quick was *that*?'

Three pairs of cold eyes stared back at her.

'What?'

'That poor calf,' said Grace.

Jess and Rosie let themselves down from the fence, looking decidedly unimpressed, and headed for the secretary's tent.

'What do you mean?' said Shara, twisting around and calling after them. 'Do you know how much skill that takes?'

She swung one leg back to dismount the fence and, as she did, her hand slipped off the smooth top rail, sending her catapulting over sideways. Her shoulder banged painfully on the rail on the way down and her feet somersaulted back over her head. She landed ungracefully, wedged against the fence, coiled over like a coffee scroll. Her lungs were so crushed inside her chest that all she could do was grunt.

As she tried to unravel herself, Corey rode past with his rope looped up and draped over Sampson's shoulder. He looked down at her with an amused glint in his eye, winked and kept riding.

'He's got tickets on himself,' grunted Jess, as she grabbed Shara by an elbow and yanked her over onto her knees. 'So much for being inconspicuous. You okay?'

Grace chortled. 'I've never seen anyone trip over their own head before!'

'Special talent,' said Shara, pulling herself up and brushing off her clothes. She turned to watch Corey's retreating back. A girl on a bay horse rode up beside him and bumped her horse against his. Corey legged Sampson over and bumped her in return. 'Hey, Mandy.'

'Is that his girlfriend?' asked Shara.

'Just some rodeo tart,' answered Grace. 'One of his many.'

'Ease up, Gracie,' said Shara. 'He could be your future brother-in-law.'

'Oh, *shut up*,' whined Grace. She always denied having a crush on Elliot, even though she had once admitted to kissing him.

'Corey rides saddle broncs too, you know,' said Jess to Shara, as though that were an unforgiveable sin.

'Oh, I didn't know that.' Shara wasn't game to admit that she liked watching the bronc riders as well.

'He's a cruel, macho, schmucky rodeo scumbag,' said Grace. 'He's nothing like his brother.'

'I can't believe they're even related,' agreed Shara. Elliot was a total geek, always tinkering with the latest techno-gadget. He wore his shirt buttoned up too high, and sneakers instead of boots. Corey, on the other hand, was more the rugged farm-boy type, always with the rolled-up shirtsleeves and big black hat. 'Since when did you guys start hating rodeo so much?'

'Since they included wild horse races,' said Jess.

Corey and his horse disappeared into a stable block and Shara watched as Mandy rode into the practice arena, raked her spurs up her horse's flanks and kicked it into a canter. When it leapt forward she gave a sharp tug on the reins.

'Ouch,' said Jess as they watched the girl pulling at her horse's mouth.

'Hey, look at the broncs,' said Shara, changing the subject. She peered into a pen full of big muscular animals, chewing slowly on hay. They were a mix of flashy colours: pinto, red roan and buckskin. A white gelding came to the fence and hung his head over it. Shara gave him a rub around the ears. 'You don't look too scary.'

Jess joined her. 'They get totally pampered, unlike the brumbies.'

The girls continued past more stock trucks and reached a wide funnel where riders entered and exited the arena. There was a small sheltered area where cowboys sat in groups alongside messy piles of helmets, vests, chaps, ropes and surcingles, waiting for their rides. Adjoining that was the secretary's tent, a large, three-sided white marquee. Through its open side, Shara could see people sitting at trestle tables tallying scores. Riders strolled in and out, checking their draw numbers and paying for their nominations.

'Hey, there are the brumbies!' said Jess, taking off. Shara and the others followed.

In another yard, several scrawny horses stood in a tight mob. Their long tangled manes ran over angular shoulders. They were a mix of sizes, some no bigger than ponies, and they looked restless and skittish. Beneath

18

their feet lay a pile of trampled hay that had been left untouched. They were a very different sight to the buck-jumpers.

'Oh, the poor things.' Jess pointed to a tall brown colt. 'Look how he spreads his legs wide to get down and graze. He's only a *baby*.'

'Surely they won't run him,' said Grace.

'I hope not,' said Jess.

A woman with a clipboard strode over to a cluster of stockmen gathered behind the chutes. She began calling names and writing things down.

'Might be time to get out of here,' said Shara. 'They're calling for teams.'

The girls found a space between the tent and the yards, and tried to blend in with the scenery.

'I want to paint the black one,' said Jess. 'She'll look great with my pink paint.' She rubbed her hands together in a scheming kind of way.

'And I'll do the creamy one,' said Grace.

'Are you guys crazy?' Shara looked around at the milling riders and stockmen. 'How are we going to get to them without anyone noticing? There are people everywhere.'

'They'll take all the men out into the arena to introduce them to the crowd,' said Jess confidently. 'We'll get about five minutes while they read all the rules and draw chute numbers out of a hat.'

A desperate, heartbreaking whinny came from the red taffy mare tethered to the semitrailer. Shara peeked out at her. The mare pawed at the ground and the hollows over her eyes pulsed with anxiety. Shara grunted in disgust, brought her can out of her pocket and gave it a shake.

'Attagirl,' said Jess, giving her a friendly nudge.

'I'll spray the grey,' sighed Rosie. 'But I want the pink paint.' She and Jess did a quick can swap.

Shara stuck her head out, gasped and pulled it in again. 'Lawson!' The girls crammed their spray cans back into their pockets.

It was an awkward moment. Grace and Rosie's older cousin ran a suspicious eye over them as he rode past on his chestnut mare, Marnie. 'What are you ratbags up to?'

'Hey, Lawson, lend us fifty bucks for some showbags!' shouted Grace.

'Fifty?' Lawson snorted. 'Think again, Gracie.' He rode away.

'That got rid of him,' said Jess.

'Look! They're grading the arena for the next event. We'll have to go really soon.' Grace rattled the can in her pocket. 'Get ready!'

In what seemed like no time at all, the competitors filed into the arena to the applause of the crowd. People ran to the sidelines to watch.

'Quick!' said Grace, stepping out towards the chutes.

The brumbies had been run into the laneway. Shara found a blue roany one, with black legs and a round belly. It snorted with fear when it saw her and banged up against the rail.

'Easy, boy, I'm not going to hurt you,' she whispered, giving the can a quick shake before spraying one word: *CRUEL*.

She threw a quick look over her shoulder – still clear – then moved to the next chute to begin spraying a red horse.

BARBAR... Damn it! She'd run out of space for the *IC*.

The horse swished its tail, smearing the last two letters. Shara stood back, looked at it and frowned. She shot a look at the others. Grace had written *HELP* across the creamy's rump, and *STOP THIS* over the ribs of a pinto. Rosie had sprayed *SAVE ME* across the grey. Shara allowed herself a giggle and took a last glance at her own work. It looked good: bold and colourful. The message was... well, nearly clear.

She turned to the others, and spotted Grace and Rosie just as they disappeared behind a market stall. Jess looked back over her shoulder and waved at Shara to hurry as she slipped after them. Just as Shara shoved the can under her jacket and prepared to leap the fence, two men emerged from the secretary's tent nearby, cutting off her escape route. Shara gasped and ducked into an empty pen, just as she recognised one of them as the man with the stockwhip. The other looked just like him, only shorter. The Conneman brothers!

'*Gone?*' the taller man shouted. 'Horses don't just disappear.'

He yanked the taffy mare's lead rope free. 'Take one of the spares, this one's wild enough.' As his brother dragged the mare towards the chutes, he yelled after him, 'And then find that stupid colt.'

'It's like Harry Houdini,' the other man grumbled.

Shara dropped to her knees behind the railings and looked desperately for a place to run. The only options were straight into the arms of the stock contractors heading her way, or to duck under the flap of the secretary's tent directly beside the pen.

The voices of the men grew louder as they drew close to her pen.

Shara made a dash for the tent flap. She rolled once and then wormed over the wet ground, under a table and into the tent.

Inside, Corey Duggin leaned against a rusty forty-four-gallon drum, one foot resting on the other, watching the queue of people in front of the secretary. He held a sheaf of entry papers for the next event.

Oh God, not him again!

For the second time that day Corey stared at her. Shara pulled herself up off the ground in the most dignified manner she could and plastered on a huge smile. 'Corey!'

'What are you *doing*?' he said with a bemused laugh.

Shara strode casually towards him past a few astonished cowboys, brushing mud from her shirt. 'We still on for the ribbon race?' she said, hoping to befuddle him.

He frowned at her, confused.

'I'll let you get the entries. Okay, then. Well. I'll see you outside.' Shara turned on her heel, walked straight out of the tent, and marched in the opposite direction from the horse yards, fiercely repressing her embarrassment.

She pushed through the shoulder-to-shoulder crowd in the sideshow alley, past the hen pavilion and around the dressage arenas. Her phone buzzed, and she whipped it out of her pocket – it was a text from Jess.

Where r u???

Shara kept walking as she messaged back.

Near the chook pav. Nice of you to wait for me.
I nearly got busted!!!

She waited for a reply.

Meet us back at the river.

Shara stuffed the phone back into her jeans pocket and took the longest and most covert route, mingling with the crowd, covering the entire perimeter of the grounds until she got to the big brick toilet block. *Phew. Made it!*

She checked to make sure the coast was clear, slipped in behind the brick wall and the cyclone fencing, squeezed through the gap – and walked straight into Corey, who was standing just outside the fence, arms folded.

'Oh. Hi, Corey.' Shara managed to find another fake smile. 'What are you doing here?'

'What are *you* doing here?'

'Ahhh...'

Corey ran his eyes up and down her, making her squirm uncomfortably. 'You're covered in cow dung.'

Shara brushed at the huge brown smears. 'I think it's just dirt.' *I hope it's just dirt.*

'Didn't know we were doing team events together today.'

'Oh yeah, that.'

He looked at her with calm hazel eyes. 'Gonna explain?'

'Umm, no.' She tried to walk around him. Corey was the enemy, a rodeoing cowboy schmuck who wasn't to be fraternised with, despite the way he filled out those jeans and that shirt so perfectly. 'But I have to cancel. I'll pay you back the entry fees.'

He blocked her path. 'I didn't pay any entry fees.'

'Oh, that's lucky.'

'Come on, Shara. You and I have both been riding in rodeos for years. What's going on? You can tell me.'

'I am *not* a rodeo rider,' she protested. 'Just because I ride in barrel races occasionally.'

'Just because you *win* barrel races occasionally,' Corey corrected her.

Shara briefly considered telling him. Corey would be okay, he was Elliot's brother. His dad was the local vet. But she pulled herself up. He was also totally pro-rodeo. He lived and breathed it.

So instead, she snorted. 'Read the paper tomorrow.' She pushed past Corey and made a bolt for the river and her waiting friends.

3

SHARA PEERED OVER her dad's shoulder at the front page of the *Coachwood Chronicle* – and nearly choked on her toast. Directly under Barry's nose was a half-page colour photo of the little roany horse, twisting and bucking against a rope with three cowboys hanging off it. The word *CRUEL* showed up perfectly against its hindquarters and rib cage.

Her mind raced back to her encounter with Corey outside the showgrounds and she cursed herself for suggesting he read this morning's paper. Now how could she deny anything? She quickly composed herself and leaned in closer to read the article.

HOOLIGANS HALT HORSE RACE

A stock contractor has vowed to prosecute activists after one of his most popular rodeo acts

was sabotaged at Coachwood Crossing Annual Show yesterday.

The wild horse race was disrupted when activists spray-painted the horses to be used in the event with the words, CRUEL, HELP and STOP.

The event calls for teams of cowboys to rope, saddle and ride wild brumbies across a finish line in the fastest time.

Stock contractor Graham Conneman said yesterday, 'The horses are well looked after and not harmed in any way. It is their natural instinct to buck. They love every minute of it.'

Anita Phillips from the Coachwood Crossing Animal Shelter disagreed. 'It is not an event that is sanctioned by official rodeo associations,' she said.

'This is all about terrorising horses for public spectacle. It is horrendously cruel.'

The shelter is calling for the Conneman brothers to surrender the brumbies so they can be rehabilitated and re-homed.

'Friends of yours, Shara?' her father asked in a dry tone.

'Mmm.' She shrugged evasively.

'I saw Don Bigwood down at the newsagent this

27

morning. He says those rodeo contractors might have some of their animals taken away from them.'

'Really?' Don Bigwood was the sergeant at the local police station.

'Yes, really. He said they're packing up so fast they're leaving skid marks.'

'Yes, well, good riddance. That wild horse race is just cruel, if you ask me.' Shara wondered whether it would look too obvious if she casually leaned over and turned the page.

Her father pointed to the photo in front of him. 'Just like it says on this horse's rump?'

'Yeah, I guess so.'

'Well, let's just hope those delinquents don't end up in a juvenile prison,' said Barry. He flipped the paper shut, and rolled it up. 'You'd never do something like that, would you?'

'Of course not!' Shara snorted.

Barry gave her a good-natured bop on the head with the rolled-up paper. 'Riding today?'

'Yep, the girls are coming over. We're going to practise sporting down on the river flats.'

'Your mum wants you to hang out the washing before you take off again. And try not to get into any mischief, hey.'

'I won't.'

Shara skipped out to the washing line, ecstatic. Not only had they shown how cruel wild horse races were, but they might have even caused the brumbies to be rescued!

Hex and Petunia let out a cacophony of howls and sprinted to greet an old Toyota Hilux with P plates that was turning into the driveway. Shara looked up from the washing basket and frowned. Corey Duggin?

The car rolled alongside the house and stopped with a crunch of the handbrake. Muffled music inside the cab cut as the engine switched off. Corey put his head out the window. 'Hi, Shara.'

'What are you doing here?'

'What are *you* doing here?'

'I live here.'

Corey stepped out of the car wearing a ragged pair of King Gee shorts, a faded T-shirt and thongs. He cast a quick glance about him.

'Looking for something?'

'Nope.' He turned his tanned face to her, his expression indifferent. 'Just dropping off strangles shots for the horses.'

'Where's Elliot?' Corey's younger brother usually did the vet deliveries.

'At a Star Trek convention or something in Brisbane. Dad said you paid for these last month, but he had none in stock then.'

'Oh yeah, that's right.'

'I can help you needle that horse of yours if you want.' He shrugged. 'While I'm here.'

Shara's first instinct was to say no. There was only one reason Corey would choose to drop off vet supplies today: he wanted to find out what had happened at the show. But Rocko was such a handful to needle – a second pair of hands *would* be good.

'Okay,' she said, a little warily. 'Just gotta finish this and then I'll catch him.'

She pegged out the last couple of shirts and then joined Corey at the yards, where she was surprised to find he'd already put a halter on Rocko. Her horse didn't usually let anyone else near him.

She took the lead rope. 'We'll have to put him in cross-ties and hobble him. He doesn't like needles.'

Corey pulled a shot out of his top pocket and un-capped it while Shara clipped a rope to either side of Rocko's halter and began buckling the restraints to his feet. 'Please be good, Rocko.'

Her horse pressed his ears back and flew at her with his teeth bared, till the chain pulled him up short. He began rearing. 'Just get it done fast,' she said to Corey.

'Hop out of the way.' Corey came in quickly to jab the needle into Rocko's neck. He pushed the plunger and pulled it out, all in less than half a second. Rocko threw his head in the air and lunged at him. 'Charming,' Corey said, as he jumped back out of the horse's reach and recapped the empty syringe.

'Sorry,' said Shara. 'He doesn't mean it.'

'So, I took your advice and read the paper this morning.'

'Did you?'

'Was that you and your mates?'

'What?'

'Who pulled the animal welfare stunt?'

Shara pulled a face at him. 'No way!'

'Even though you thought today's paper might be worth a read?'

Shara bent down and unbuckled the hobbles around Rocko's feet, avoiding his eyes. 'Nup.'

'The contractors have surrendered the brumbies.'

Shara looked up at him. 'Are you for real?'

Corey smiled down at her and his face seemed genuine and kind. 'Yeah. I just heard about it from Dad.'

'That's fantastic! They'll be saved.' She couldn't hide her delight.

'Thought I'd stop in and give you the goss. Just in case, you know, you might know anyone who was involved in it. Which you . . . don't?'

She shook her head. 'No.'

'It's not a good event, that wild horse race. It gives rodeo a bad name.'

Shara looked into Corey's hazel-brown eyes and won-dered why he was telling her this. Did he agree with what she had done or was he trying to get enough information to pin it on her? Best keep her mouth shut, she decided. He was still connected to a lot of other rodeo people who did not share the same views, and word spread quickly in horsey circles. She watched him run a hand over Rocko's back. Her horse certainly seemed to trust him, though, and that was very unusual.

'You doing the Nanango draft next weekend?' she asked, buckling the hobbles back together and changing the subject.

'Yep. You?'

'Don't know yet. Dad's car is at the mechanic's. Not sure if it'll be fixed by then.'

'I've got a spare spot on the float.' Corey looked out over the paddocks where the cattle grazed, then gave her a wink. 'We can train on your cattle this week.'

She smiled back. Now he was getting cheeky. 'Those ones are all pregnant. Dad would spew.'

'Doesn't he have to draft out some weaners or some-thing?'

'He did that last week.'

'Bummer. Come to the draft anyway.'

'What about all the other girls I see you with?'

He rolled his eyes. 'It's not easy being a demigod.'

'Might be a bit too squeezy on that horse float.'

'Come with me anyway,' said Corey. 'Just as a friend.'

Shara shook her head. Corey might seem nice enough, but he was still a rodeo boy who roped calves and rode bucking broncos. He didn't fit with her crowd of friends. 'I'll make my own way there.'

As Corey's Hilux rolled out of the driveway, Grace and Jess rode in.

'What's *he* doing here?' asked Jess, after giving Corey a perfunctory wave. 'You didn't tell him anything, did you?'

'No.'

'Did he ask?'

'Sort of. I just brushed it off,' Shara said reassuringly.

'He's already pummelled Elliot for information,' said Grace, slipping off her horse and tying it to the hitching rail.

'Did Elliot tell?'

'No,' said Grace. 'But he reckons Corey really hammered him.'

'Typical rodeo thug,' said Jess dismissively. 'Hey, did you see the picture in the *Coachwood Chronicle*?' She jumped off Dodger and pulled a folded piece of newspaper from her pocket. 'We're famous!'

'Infamous, you mean,' said Shara. 'I nearly choked on my breakfast when Dad opened the paper this morning.'

'Our mum loved it,' said Rosie.

'She would have done the spray-painting herself,' said Grace, 'but the Connemans already have a restraining order against her. Just about every stock contractor in the country does. I think she thumped one of them once.'

Shara laughed. She could just imagine Mrs Arnold, with her mad black curly hair and fiery tongue, hammering the head of a scrawny cowboy. If only her own parents were that cool.

'I drove past the show this morning with Mum and the red semitrailer was gone. They'd packed all the yards and signs away,' said Jess.

'Corey told me they surrendered the brumbies,' said Shara excitedly. 'They'll be re-homed instead of being turned into pet food.'

'Oh! That's fantastic,' said Grace. 'Wow! We saved some brumbies! That's so freaking good!'

'Corey's okay, I reckon,' said Shara.

'No, he's *not*,' said Jess. 'He strings along about ten girlfriends at once, and he rides broncos. Don't let him charm you, Shara. He's a cowboy schmuck!'

'I'm not letting him charm me! I just said he's okay. He's not as bad as you think.'

Jess pulled a face. '*Anyway*, those dodgy Conneman

brothers probably won't be coming back to Coachwood Crossing again. Saddle up, Sharsy. Let's ride.'

Shara skipped to the shed to get her saddle, her friends following. The tin door was flapping open, and she hooked it back against the wall, puzzled. 'It's not like Dad to leave the door open.'

She headed into the shed, and stopped in her tracks. Inside, the two wooden racks that held her saddles and rugs stood empty. Around her feet lay a mess of leather and canvas.

Hex leapt about and sniffed urgently, darting from one bundle to the next. He investigated an old chaff bag that lay emptied on the floor. Then he trotted the length of the workbench, inspecting the boxes of nails and screws and David's tools that lay strewn beneath.

'What happened to the shed?' asked Jess.

'It's been ransacked,' answered Shara.

She bent down and picked up her pride and joy, the trophy saddle she'd won at the Longwood campdraft finals. 'Oh no! It's all scratched.' She replaced it carefully on the rack. 'Who would go through all my stuff like that?'

4

SERGEANT BIGWOOD came over that afternoon and took a statement from Shara, but said as nothing had been stolen there was little he could do. 'Just local kids up to no good,' he had concluded, and Shara's dad had agreed.

Shara wasn't convinced. She lay awake that night, fretting. Who would have done such a horrible thing? Did someone have a grudge against her? She tried to think about something else. School. Biology. She loved biology. It was full of all sorts of stuff that she could relate to horses, such as reproductive systems and genetics. She had learned, for instance, that if she put a cremello stallion over a bay mare, she could get a buckskin foal. She got an A+ for that assignment.

As she drifted towards sleep, a strange ruckus, like steel on steel, started outside. Shara lifted her head from the pillow and held her breath, listening. There it was again. But why weren't the dogs barking?

Shara jumped out of bed and ran to her parents' room. Barry met her in the hallway.

'Did you hear that, Dad?'

'It sounded like the shed door,' he said. 'You stay in the house and I'll check it out.'

'Let the dogs off,' she whispered. 'They'll sort it out.'

'No, I want to catch this troublemaker in the act.' Her father marched off, pulled on his boots and grabbed a baseball bat from behind the front door.

'Be careful, Dad!'

'I'll be fine. It's probably just some kid. Don't turn any lights on for a bit.' He stopped and turned to her. 'Stay here,' he ordered. Then he slipped out the door and disappeared into the front yard.

Shara's mum joined her at the lounge-room window, drawing a robe tightly around herself and tying the belt. Together, they squinted into the darkness.

Within seconds, Barry was back. 'Call the police, Louise. I reckon there's more than one of them in there, not just kids by the noise.'

'What did you hear? What are they doing?'

'Not sure, but they're making a hell of a racket. Don't seem to care who hears them.'

Shara frowned, puzzled. Why were the dogs so quiet?

'The police are on their way,' said Louise from behind them. 'I think you should just wait and let them handle it, Barry. There's no point you getting hurt.'

'Fine by me,' he agreed.

For ten minutes there was no sound from the shed but an occasional jingle of saddlery. Then blue flashing lights lit the surrounding paddocks and a car tore up the gravel road towards the house. Hex and Petunia went berserk. From the shed came an explosion of metal and concrete. The shed door slammed.

Barry ran across the yard to greet the police car. 'They just took off!'

Don Bigwood leapt from the car and followed Barry into the darkness, gripping a torch. Voices yelled and twigs snapped. Streaks of light waved about in the bushes. Louise snapped on the verandah lights.

The men were back at the house within five minutes. Barry held his palms in the air, panting. 'They were like ninjas.'

Don Bigwood shrugged. 'Disappeared into thin air.'

Hex whined from his kennel. 'Shut up, you useless dog,' Shara growled at him.

Again, she found the shed in a mess. One of the saddles had been knocked to the floor and the chaff bag had been gone through again. This time, however, the door to the feedroom was also ajar. Oats and barley carpeted the floor.

'Looks more like an animal has broken in to get at the feed,' said the sergeant. 'One of your cows, maybe.'

'But we shut the doors with two barrel bolts,' said Shara. 'No animal could open that.' She looked around her. 'There are no droppings. A cow would leave poo everywhere.' She began to pick up her stuff, frowning.

After the sergeant left, Barry re-bolted the doors. He made sure the windows were closed and secured them with timber rods. 'Let's just hope they've found what they're looking for and will leave us alone from now on.'

Shara brought her saddles back to the house, just to be on the safe side. Before she turned off her bedside lamp for the second time that night, she thumbed a quick message to Jess.

Shed broken into again, meet @ bakery early.

The next morning Shara sat in the main street outside the bakery, inhaling the delicious aroma of hot bread. Hex and Petunia panted lazily at her feet. She looked at her watch: six-thirty. Maybe Jess wasn't working today. She had already earned enough to pay for her new filly, Opal. Maybe she could no longer cope with selling stodgy white carbohydrates and had cut back on shifts. Shara pulled her phone from her bag and thumbed another message:

She decided to go in and buy a lime-green doughnut while she was waiting. At this hour of the morning, they'd be hot from the fryer. She could scoff it before Jess arrived to lecture her about the evils of artificial colourings and high GI.

A bell ding-a-linged as Shara pulled open the flyscreen door and stepped into the yeasty warmth of the bakery. She smiled hello to Jess's boss, who was busily bundling up two large bags of bread for a customer. 'Hi, Chan. Jess working today?'

'She should be here any minute,' answered Chan. As she spoke, the man she'd been serving tucked a bag under each arm and came away from the counter. He was tall and broad-shouldered, with a lean face that seemed somehow familiar. Nudging the door open with his elbow, he squeezed out. There was a high-pitched yelp from outside.

'Hey!' Shara yelled after him. 'Don't kick my dog!'

'Put the mongrel on a leash,' muttered the man, without turning around.

Shara's mouth formed a huge, incensed *O*. Hex and Petunia were totally well-behaved. Who was this out-of-towner to tell her what to do with her dogs? 'Big man,' she said sarcastically, loud enough for it to feel good, but

40

not quite loud enough for him to hear. 'Feel good to kick a defenceless animal, does it?'

'It probably does, to him,' said Jess, appearing behind her. 'He's one of the Conneman brothers.' She threw her bag down behind the counter and tied an apron around her back.

'How do you know?'

'I get all the gossip in here. He's been coming in and getting the day-old bread to feed the horses. Yesterday he parked the Bred to Buck truck out the front.'

'I thought they'd left town.'

'They must have some *unfinished business*.'

Shara felt an uneasy gnawing in her gut.

Jess took a crate of hot bread and carried it across the shop to arrange the loaves neatly on the shelves. 'So what happened last night at your place?'

Shara filled her in on the night's events. 'Sergeant Bigwood thought it might be a cow or something trying to get at the feed, but the door had two barrel bolts holding it closed.'

'Well, that guy was pretty big,' said Jess, tilting her head out towards the street, as a small red car eased out of its parking spot and rolled down the main street.

Shara squirmed at the thought. 'How would he know who I was or where I lived?' She paused. 'Do you think he *might* know I was part of the protest?'

Jess shrugged.

'Hex would've barked if it was a person.' Shara wished she could feel a little more certain of that.

'You're probably right. Unless it was someone Hex knows.' Jess paused. 'It wouldn't be Corey, would it? It was a bit weird how he came over to your house the other day.'

'He came to tell me the brumbies had been rescued,' said Shara. 'He was being nice.'

Jess arched an eyebrow. 'Sure?'

'No.' Shara couldn't hide her uncertainty. When she thought of Corey's easy smile, she was sure. But when she thought of his rodeo career and hard-handed girlfriends, she became decidedly unsure.

5

THAT NIGHT, Shara lay in bed with her hands gripped tightly around her dad's giant spotlight. In the paddock beyond the window, two round-bellied cows lumbered down the hillside. More followed, breaking into a jog along the steep track that carved through the property. Had something disturbed them?

Shara stared hard into the darkness. Then, somewhere closer to the house, there was a low groan. Hex growled. Then silence.

Slowly, carefully, Shara slid the window open and listened. She heard a low whine and then a grunt. It didn't fit the usual night-time noises. Shara was startled to see a large dark shape near her brother's dead cars.

She tiptoed hurriedly to her parents' bedroom door. 'Dad,' she whispered. 'There's something moving down in the front yard. It's really big.'

'Well, there's your burglar,' he said, pushing aside the

quilt and reaching for a robe. He made his way to the door. 'Got your torch?'

Shara flicked the spotlight on and cast sweeping beams of light over the front yard. Hex immediately whined. Petunia let out a small yap. There was a rustle of bushes. 'There!' she hissed. 'By the shed!'

Two red eyes glimmered in the torchlight. Then something groaned and dropped heavily to the ground.

The verandah lights snapped on.

'A horse,' gasped Shara.

Startled by the sudden light, it scrambled to its feet and staggered sideways, placing itself back in the shadows of the garden, with its legs wide apart and its head low. Streaks of light from the verandah played on the silvery spangles of its mane.

But it was in trouble. It stood with flaring nostrils before lowering itself to the ground and rolling wildly with its legs in the air.

'It's a colt! He's got colic or something,' said Shara, running down the front steps with bare feet. 'We need a halter!'

'You keep an eye on him, love. I'll get one from the shed.' Barry disappeared into the darkness.

Shara approached the horse slowly. 'Easy, boy.'

The horse lay on his side and looked up at her, then curled his neck to look at his stomach.

44

'I don't know who undid the barrel bolts for him, but he's been into the feedroom,' said Barry, reappearing with a halter. 'There's hay and grain everywhere.'

'No wonder he has a bellyache.' The horse groaned as Shara pulled the halter over his ears. 'It's okay, boy, I'm not gonna hurt you.' She gave him a gentle pull and urged him to walk. 'Better get up and keep moving, otherwise your gizzards'll get twisted.'

She pulled at the colt's head with all her strength until he struggled to his feet. He took one reluctant step after another and then pushed his head into her tummy as though begging her to stop. A long moan rumbled from his chest.

'Oh, you poor thing,' she said, noticing the patches of sweat on his neck and over his eyes. 'He needs a vet, Dad.'

'Can't it wait till morning?'

'I don't think he'll still be alive by then.'

The colt crumpled to the ground again and threw back his head, thrashing his legs. Shara pulled at the rope. 'No, no, you have to get up!' She had the awful feeling that he might never rise again if she let him stay down. 'Dad, this is an emergency!'

Barry groaned. 'Why do these things always happen in the middle of the night? Don't horses know that vets charge double to make midnight calls?'

'Mum, help me!'

Louise pulled on some boots and ran down the steps in her robe. 'You pull his head. I'll get his tail.' She grabbed the horse's ratty, half-chewed tail and gave it a good firm yank. He put one leg out in front of him and lifted his head. 'That's it, come on,' encouraged Shara. 'Give him a kick, Mum.'

Louise gave the horse a few encouraging nudges on the rump with her foot. 'Come on,' she said, in a no-nonsense voice. 'Up!'

Shara was massively relieved when the colt struggled to his feet again. 'I'll try to bring him into the light,' she said, dragging him closer to the house. Under the verandah's spotlight, the colt was so thin that his ribs stuck out along his back. His shoulders were flat and triangular and his flanks sank away from his hip bones. 'He's an RSPCA case. Look at him!'

Barry let out a sigh and headed up the steps to the back door. 'One big vet bill coming up.'

Shara half-led, half-dragged the colt around under the light to keep him moving while they waited for the vet and, as she did, she noticed something very interesting about him. His coat was a burnt golden-brown and there were black dapples on his hindquarters. His mane was silver, almost white.

This colt was a silver taffy, which gave Shara a

powerful clue about where he had come from. She'd learned when researching her biology assignment that only a red taffy crossed with a black could produce a horse of that colouring. Her mind raced back to the frantic taffy mare, tied to the semi. This had to be her colt. The older Conneman's words rang in her ears. *Find that stupid colt!*

Shara kept walking and talked soothingly to the little horse. 'You must be a tricky fellow to get into my feed bins. No need to ask how you got colic!'

Barry trotted down the stairs looking quite jolly for a man who'd just committed himself to a second mortgage. 'John Duggin is on his way. He said he'll be half an hour and to keep the horse walking.' He surprised Shara by smiling. 'He said that if we ring the RSPCA in the morning and surrender the horse, they'll cover the bill until they track down the owner.'

Shara couldn't help feeling a bit disappointed. There was something special about this little guy. She had the same feeling about him she'd had when she first saw Rocko. There was some sort of reason why their paths had crossed. She loved nursing animals back to health, and knew in her heart that this horse would be much better off with her than with its current owners.

Shara was still with the colt when the RSPCA arrived the next morning. Her legs ached and she was so tired she thought her head might drop off.

John Duggin had put a tube into one of the colt's nostrils and down into its stomach. Then he'd poured paraffin oil down to flush out any blockages. He gave the colt a needle to stop the spasms and told Shara to keep walking him until he did a poo. The poos came just as the sun was rising. Boy, did they come. With great relief, Shara had unclipped the colt and retreated a safe distance to let him do his business.

A few hours later, a white RSPCA van pulled into the driveway. Two women got out, looking very official with clipboards under their arms. 'Shara Wilson?' asked the more matronly of the two.

'Yes,' said Shara, holding out her hand.

'Lurlene Spencer.'

'And I'm Anita from the animal shelter,' said the younger woman, stepping forward with a smile. 'We often work together.'

Lurlene stepped past them both and looked at the colt. 'Is this the horse you reported?' She turned and glared at Shara as if she were responsible for the colt's suffering.

'It ate nearly a whole bag of barley and then we found it last night with colic.'

'Well, no wonder if it gorged itself on grain, especially

48

when it's malnourished like that,' the woman snorted.

'Oh, hello? I'm the one who has been dragging myself around all night keeping the poor animal alive! Our shed door had two barrel bolts on it, so it was hardly our fault.' Shara was tired and hungry and worried about the colt. She didn't need the third degree as well.

'I see.' Lurlene Spencer opened her clipboard and began to take notes. 'We'll call him Goldie, shall we?'

The younger woman caught Shara's eye and pulled a face that seemed to say, *You should try working with her all day!*

'We got the vet out and he's treated him with paraffin oil and anti-spasm drugs,' said Shara, trying to stay polite. 'And I walked him most of the night. He had a big poo at about five-thirty this morning.'

'Yes, yes, we received the vet's report by fax this morning,' Lurlene said in a dismissive tone. She unbuckled the gate and entered the yard. 'There's still a very high risk of founder.' She ran a hand down the colt's shoulder and spoke softly to him before stepping back and taking more notes. 'And you don't know who owns Goldie?'

Shara hesitated. 'Will they take him back if you find them?'

'Hardly. They'll be lucky not to be prosecuted. If I have anything to do with it, they will be. Do you have the camera, Anita? We'll need some pictures.'

'I think I have an idea who he might belong to,' offered Shara.

'Yes?'

'He might belong to the rodeo contractors who just left town: the Conneman brothers.'

The women looked at each other and then at her. 'What makes you think it's theirs?' asked Anita.

'Well, this colt is a silver taffy, and . . .'

'It's a palomino, dear,' Lurlene corrected.

What is your problem?

'Actually, it's not. Silver taffies are often confused with palominos.' Shara spoke quickly before she was incorrectly corrected again. 'See those black dapples on his hindquarters? Well, they can only come from crossing a red taffy with a black. So one of its parents must be a red taffy, which isn't very common.'

Both women looked totally gripped now, obviously dazzled by her expertise on equine genetics.

'And when I was at the Coachwood Crossing Show the other day . . .' *Doh! Did I just admit that?* ' . . . I noticed a red taffy mare tied to the Connemans' truck, and she was whinnying like she'd just lost her foal. This horrible man came out from behind the truck and whipped her. He was very cruel.'

'Yes, we're familiar with the Conneman brothers and their training methods,' said Anita. 'Actually, there was a protest staged there a few days ago, quite a successful one. It gained a bit of media coverage and it may lead to further investigations.' She looked the colt up and down and added thoughtfully, 'The Connemans did leave the area in a hurry. Maybe they left this animal behind in their haste.'

'So what will happen to him?' asked Shara, resisting an urge to boast that she had been involved in the protest.

'He'll be taken back to the shelter and rehabilitated,' said Lurlene. 'If we can prove that he's been neglected or cruelly treated, which shouldn't be difficult in this case, we can prosecute.'

'Then what will happen to him?'

'He'll be placed in a suitable home.'

'So is there any chance of him staying with the current carer?' asked Shara. 'Could I look after him here?'

Lurlene hesitated. 'Possibly. You wouldn't be able to charge the previous owner for costs, though. Only the RSPCA can do that.' She looked at the colt. 'He needs proper veterinary treatment. He's quite a mess.'

Shara's shoulders slumped. There was no way her dad would pay a load of vet bills for a horse he didn't own, especially when the RSPCA was willing to do so.

Anita looked out into the grazing paddock, which was knee-high in lush green pasture. She eyed Rocko, who grazed alongside Louise's big mare, Bella. Both were shiny and healthy. 'Or we could take him back to the shelter, stabilise him and then bring him back here to fatten up. You would need to register yourself as a volunteer, though.'

Shara's heart leapt. Now that was a plan she could work with!

'We would need your parents' consent, though. You are under eighteen?' said Lurlene.

'Well, yes. Umm, you may need to talk to Dad.'

A hint of a smile crossed Lurlene's lips.

Whatever the two women said to Barry, it worked miracles. Shara watched from a distance as Lurlene and Anita smiled, chatted, joked and charmed his mismatched footy socks off. By the time they stepped off the front verandah and rejoined her by the yard, they were making arrangements to pick up Goldie and drop him back a few days later.

That afternoon, Shara helped Anita load the colt into the float and although he looked weak and tired, he walked up the ramp without fuss. He had obviously been on a float before.

As she watched the car and float roll out of the drive-way, she fizzed with excitement. In only a couple of days, she might have a new horse – a gorgeous silver taffy!

6

ON SATURDAY, Shara lay in the hammock on the back verandah impatiently tapping her boots together. She'd attempted to read some science papers for an upcoming assignment, but she could barely focus.

It had been a whole forty-eight hours since she'd heard any news of the colt. Had he recovered fully? Horses could be sick for weeks after grain colic, and Goldie was in such poor condition to start with. Why wouldn't John Duggin answer his phone?

She sighed and looked out to where Rocko grazed in the long grass. It was an unbelievably gorgeous morning and it seemed criminal to be sitting around and not riding. But Jess had to work at the bakery all morning, and Shara had promised she would wait for her.

After reprimanding herself repeatedly for even thinking of the idea, Shara finally decided that she might as well ring the rodeo schmuck. Corey worked for his dad part-time. He might know something.

How to get his number? Ask Elliot? But he'd tell Grace, Grace would tell Jess, and Jess could be such a disapproving old woman. Hmmm. Shara pulled out her iPhone and googled the local branch of the rodeo assoc- iation, then scrolled through its contacts. *Aha!*

'How's the draft?' she asked when he picked up. Much cooler not to introduce herself.

'Good cattle,' said Corey on the other end. 'Purebred Droughtmasters. You'd like them.' Shara could hear their crooning in the background mingling with country music and instantly wished she was there.

'So, did you find someone to share the float?'

'No. I was saving a spot for you.'

'Do you even know who this is?'

'Of course I do.'

She remained silent, testing him. Grace reckoned he had so many girlfriends he couldn't keep up with them all.

'Shara,' he said, after the smallest of pauses.

'Took you a while.'

'I've got one more run in the Novice, then I'm done for the day. You should come out for the band tonight.'

He was incorrigible, which she found kind of enjoy- able. But she remained aloof. 'Can't, I promised I'd go on a night ride with Jess.' That was close enough to the truth – give or take a few hours.

'You can ride around in the dark all you like out here.'

'Not quite the same,' she said. 'Hey, did your dad tell you about the colt that showed up at my place?'

'The one you thought was a burglar?'

'Err, yes.' It seemed so stupid now. Best not to tell Corey that at one stage she had thought *he* might be the burglar. 'Your dad came and looked at him. Have you heard anything about how he's going?'

'He's at the Coachwood Animal Shelter. They're having trouble with him.'

'Why, what's wrong?' asked Shara. 'Has he been sick again?'

'No, but he's badly undernourished. Dad reckons he's about two years old, from the look of his teeth. He's only as big as a yearling, though. But that's not the trouble.'

'So, what is?'

'He can undo stable doors. He chews on anything; lead ropes, brushes. He chewed the back pocket off my jeans while I was talking to one of the staff. Cheeky.' Corey sounded suddenly distracted. 'Hey, I gotta go and warm up. Talk later, hey?'

'Okay, bye.' Shara imagined him on that big red quarter horse, tucking his phone back in his pocket, kicking it into a canter and circling a few laps. He looked good on a horse. No wonder girls hung off him all the time. Not her, though – Corey was *so* not her type.

She lay there basking in the sunshine and hummed a little tune. Her dad walked onto the verandah and set a cup of coffee and the newspaper on the table.

'I just visited Goldie at the shelter,' said Barry. 'The staff say he's doing great.'

'Did you?' Shara peered over the lip of the hammock, surprised. 'I just spoke to Corey, and *he* says he's been undoing stable doors.'

'Hmmm.' Barry began flipping through the paper. 'They didn't tell me that bit.'

Shara wondered whether to tell him about the rest of the colt's antics and decided against it. 'Have they found the owners yet?'

'No – the RSPCA's been in touch with the Connemans, and they denied owning him. But they're probably just trying to avoid prosecution.' He took a sip of his coffee.

'Oh. So what happens next? Where will Goldie end up?'

'Well, if they can't prove he belongs to the Connemans, they'll find him a new home.'

'He could come and live here, Dad. He could be your horse,' said Shara, the idea coming to her and flowing out of her mouth before she could register how stupid it was.

Shara's mother walked onto the verandah. Her gold

bracelets jingled as she set a platter of sandwiches on the table. 'What? Haven't we got enough big mouths to feed around here?'

'Well, actually—' Barry began.

'Actually what?' said Louise. 'You don't even like riding, Barry.'

'I was thinking more about when Rocko goes,' said Barry. 'If Shara retires him some day, she'll have nothing to ride. Be good for her to have a young one coming through.'

Shara's mouth fell open.

Barry continued. 'Of course, there's still the chance that the Connemans *are* telling the truth and that somebody else owns him. But if the RSPCA can prove he belonged to them, they can send them the colt's feed and vet bills and then re-home him.'

Shara couldn't believe it. She would have her own project horse to train and break in. Her dad was talking as if they already owned Goldie! She leapt out of the hammock and gave her dad a huge squeeze. 'You are the best dad in the whole world!'

He patted her arm. 'Nothing's final yet, but if we get him, he can be your birthday pressie.'

She hugged him even tighter.

'Just don't let it distract you from your studies,' Louise put in. 'You're doing so well right now.'

'I promise!'

Shara was so wound up with excitement she barely knew what to do with herself. She couldn't wait for Jess to finish work at the bakery so she could tell her. Eventually, she wandered down the hill paddock to check on the cows.

She sat by the creek's edge imagining what Goldie would look like grazing alongside Rocko. She pictured him trotting up for his feed and giving her a friendly whinny, the way Jess's horse Dodger always did for her. Goldie was so sweet and gentle, unlike Rocko. Much as she loved her big quarter horse, they got along best when she was on his back. It would be soooo nice to have a horse who enjoyed a pat.

She began planning his training schedule. If he was two years old, she could start lunging and mouthing already! She would need a good lead horse. Maybe Jess would let her borrow Dodger. There were so many things to teach Goldie. He was beginning to feel like her horse already!

7

THREE DAYS LATER, Shara thought she might totally explode with anticipation. It seemed like months since her brief encounter with Goldie, and she could barely remember what he looked like. Her friends had come to help get everything ready for his arrival.

'Did they find Goldie's owners yet?' asked Grace, as she helped Shara spread fresh new bales of straw about the stable.

'Nah,' said Shara. 'But I reckon the Connemans owned him for sure.'

'I googled them, and from what I found, they definitely did.' Jess carried two huge armfuls of hay from the shed and stuffed them into the manger.

'What did you find?'

'According to their website, they supply cattle for rough riding events,' said Jess. 'There were heaps of buckjumping photos. One rider even looked like Corey.' She shot Shara a censorious look.

'Did he have gorgeous brown hair and eyes to die for?' asked Shara, just to stir up her bestie.

Jess threw Shara a disgusted look. 'I don't know, he had a big stupid rodeo hat on. Anyway, they reckoned they used real outback brumbies, *wild and untamed*, and they had heaps of photos of the wild horse race. There were a couple of that red taffy mare too. You know, the one tied to their truck that day.' She picked up two empty buckets from the corner of the stable and walked to the door.

'So, she *was* a brumby.'

'*Apparently*.' Jess turned back to her friends and lowered her voice. 'They also had a black quarter horse stallion imported from America, and there was a photo of him in a neck-stretch gallop with a rider hanging off one side. He's a trick-riding horse. Very cool.'

'Ha!' said Shara. 'I knew it! Mix a red taffy with a black and what do you get? A silver taffy! Goldie belonged to them!'

'Here he comes!' shouted Grace, pointing to the horse float barrelling along the road behind Barry's car. The girls ran to open the front gate. A faint whinny sounded from inside the float as it turned into the driveway.

Barry pulled up, walked to the back of the float and

let the tailgate down. The colt shifted about anxiously, banging against the chain that looped behind his rump.

Shara ran to the front of the float and pulled the door open. Goldie tossed his head and sniffed at her. 'Heyyy,' she said, holding out an open hand for him to nuzzle. 'Remember me?'

She ran both hands over his cheeks and looked into his big, soft eyes. The colt tossed his head again. 'Yes, I think you do!'

Shara reached to untie him and found a soggy stump dangling from the tie-hook. 'Hey! You've chewed through your lead rope.'

Barry poked his head through the other front door. 'He's been through a few of them. The staff at the shelter just gave up and used baling twine – it was getting too expensive. He's good at getting his halter off, too, if it's not done up firmly.'

Shara shrugged. 'Doesn't matter, we'll sort something out.' She called out to Jess, who stood ready to unhook the rear chain. 'Okay, let him off!'

The colt backed carefully down the ramp and then let out a long neigh as if to announce his own important arrival. Shara looked him over. He really was the most amazing burnt gold, with the black dapples down his hindquarters and hocks, and his thick, silvery mane. He'd lost his wormy belly, and Shara could see the muscle definition so typical of a quarter horse. Even though he was still so thin, she could see he would be spectacular; way beyond anything she had hoped for.

'Come on, handsome,' she said, pulling at what was left of his rope. 'Come and see your new home.' She led him into the yard, unclipped him and watched as Rocko galloped up from the adjoining paddock. The two horses stood, necks arched over the fence, puffing into each other's nostrils. Rocko let out a shrill squeal and struck out with his front leg. Goldie immediately lashed back. Although half Rocko's size, he kept squealing and striking.

'I think he has short-man syndrome,' laughed Jess.

'He's cheeky,' said Shara. 'Lucky there's a good strong fence between them or Rocko would give him a hiding!'

The colt turned his back on Rocko and paced around the yard, inspecting everything. He walked into the shelter and nosed through the straw bedding, took a nibble of the hay and waggled his lips in the water. He picked up one of Shara's new brushes in his teeth, a mischievous look in his eye. Then he trotted back out with his tail in the air and shook his head, tossing the brush to the other side of the yard.

'Hey!' said Shara. 'That's my new brush you're flinging about!' She retrieved it and resumed her seat on the rail with her friends.

Goldie pushed the water bucket with his nose and tipped it over, making a big puddle. The girls watched in disbelief as he took the bucket in his teeth and carried it over to the fence. Rocko stopped squealing and sniffed the bucket through the railings.

Jess squealed with laughter. 'He's trying to offer Rocko a bribe!'

'A peace offering,' said Rosie.

'Wow, maybe it's true about the trick-horse bloodlines,' said Shara. 'I think that black stallion has passed on his trickery to this guy!'

'Look what he's doing now,' said Jess.

The colt put the bucket on the ground and, using his nose and one hoof, he flipped it upside-down. Then, one hoof at a time, he stepped up onto the bucket.

'Look at that!' said Shara.

Grace began to clap. 'Clever boy!'

Rocko snorted and stepped back a pace, as Goldie carefully moved his hind legs about, one by one, and lined himself up with the fence. He lifted a hind leg in the air and searched for the bucket.

'Uh, oh!' said Shara, leaping off the fence. 'I think he has an even better trick in mind.'

Before she could grab his halter, Goldie had all four feet balanced precariously on the metal bucket. As it began to buckle under his weight, he half pounced, half scrambled over the fence. The girls watched, open-mouthed, as he landed on the other side in a clatter of hooves.

Goldie braced his legs beneath him and shook like a dog, as if ridding himself of the yard once and for all. He paused momentarily to take in his new surroundings, then burst into a gallop, squealing and grunting, tail in the air. Rocko snorted and followed, his tail upright and waving like a banner.

'Wowww,' said Grace in an awestruck voice. 'He's a freak.' She looked at Shara, eyes full of excitement.

'He's a complete nightmare,' said Shara. 'How am I going to keep him in?' She reached for a halter and began walking down the paddock. 'How am I even going to catch him?'

Grace ran after her. 'All the good ones take a bit more effort, Shara. That's what Mum says. The only thing standing between a smart horse and the knacker's yard is good training!'

'I think he needs un-training!' said Shara. 'Look at him!' The colt was careering around the paddock with his nose in the air, making a complete mockery of her. Rocko frolicked alongside him, sharing in the joke.

'I've never seen such a smart horse,' said Rosie, jogging after them.

'He is *so* beautiful.' Grace stared, love-struck, after the colt. 'You are *so* lucky.'

'Lucky?' What on earth was she going to do with a horse that could jump shoulder-high fences?

It took quite a bit of talking to convince Shara's father of Goldie's freakish talents and the need for electric fencing. In the end Barry went to buy some tape and insulators just to get her off his case. Then he spent the afternoon helping the girls to screw little plastic rings to the top of the fence and thread electric tape through it.

Shara stood back and regarded the white strip that ran the perimeter of the yard. 'That should keep him in,' she said with her hands on her hips. She felt much better.

'Well, it'll do as a temporary solution,' said Barry. 'But he can't live in a pen his whole life, Shara. You'll have to train him to stay inside fences.'

'Of course, good training, that's what he needs.' But Shara wasn't at all sure how she would do that. Goldie could also undo gates. They'd have to padlock everything.

'Maybe he'll settle down after a week or so,' said Grace. 'He's probably never stayed in one place for long. The contractors always had him on the move.' She patted Goldie's neck. 'You've never had a real home, have you, mate?'

Shara wished she could feel as optimistic. 'Maybe he

just needs a routine. Horses love routine. They're creatures of habit.' She took the power box in her hand. 'Stand clear.'

'Clear,' they all chorused, stepping away from the white tape. It clicked intermittently as the current pulsed through it.

Shara let Goldie go in the yard again. 'Fingers crossed.'

Goldie sniffed at the air and remained still for a while, ears flicking about, picking up the click of the tape. After moseying around the inner yard for a while, he eventually sighed, walked into the shelter and busied himself with the hay, pulling big tufts from the manger and chewing contentedly.

'That seems to be working,' said Shara, breathing a sigh of relief. 'He's not going anywhere near it.'

'Here comes Mum,' said Grace suddenly. 'Wait till she sees him.'

Mrs Arnold's four-wheel drive rolled up behind them. She hung an elbow out the window. 'Geez, you've got him fenced in like Fort Knox.'

'We had to,' said Grace, running over to the window. 'You should see how clever he is at getting out. He jumps on buckets!'

'What do you mean, he jumps on buckets?'

'He picks them up in his teeth and then uses them like a stepladder to get out.'

'You need to geld him,' said Mrs Arnold. 'That'll settle him. Cuts out a bit of their brains, but he's got a few to spare by the sound of it.'

'Of course!' said Shara. Mrs Arnold was a genius! Colts were always a bit mischievous. As soon as she cleared gelding with the RSPCA, all would be fine!

8

SHARA WOKE TO the sound of the telephone.

'Oh, dear,' she could hear her mother saying. 'Mr Hickling, I'm terribly sorry . . . Yes . . . Yes . . . Oh dear. I really am sorry. I'll send Shara straight away.'

'Oh God!' Shara leapt from her bed and rushed to Louise as she hung up the phone. 'What happened? Who was that?'

'It's Goldie again,' said Louise shortly. 'Mr Hickling found him in his orchard this morning. He's devoured two tubs of lychees and damaged some of the trees.'

Shara groaned. 'How did he get out this time?'

'I don't know, love. But you'd better find a way to keep him in or he'll have to go back to the RSPCA. We don't want to get offside with the neighbours.'

Shara's heart sank. 'But the RSPCA only have stables! That's why they sent him here, so he could get out and graze. He needs to stretch his legs and be with other

68

horses, otherwise he might as well be tied to a contractor's truck all day.'

'Maybe, but I don't know what else you can do. He can't just roam the neighbourhood at will.'

'Just give him one more chance. Please? I'll go and collect him and then I'll check the electric wire. Maybe it shorted out on some grass or something.'

Shara threw on some old clothes, took a halter from the shed and walked up the road to the Hickling property. In the orchard, among the big, glossy lychee trees, fruit pickers stood on ladders tossing handfuls of red fruit into plastic tubs. As she approached, Shara could see Goldie's scrawny rump at the end of a row. His head was deep in a plastic tub, and there was a mess of skins and pips trampled beneath his feet. He looked up at her with a face full of slobber, well pleased with himself.

'He's been having a fine feast on my lychees, the little so-and-so,' said a voice from behind her. She spun around. Mr Hickling stood there in a green apron, holding a pair of cutters in his hand.

'Oh, I'm so sorry, Mr Hickling. I'll pay for the fruit you've lost,' said Shara.

'No need this time,' he said, softening. 'But see that he doesn't get out again, hey? He's had a good old scratch on my trees and broken off some branches. I can't afford any more damage like that.'

'I promise it won't happen again,' said Shara, slipping a halter over Goldie's head. She pulled the reluctant colt away from the tub, deeply embarrassed.

'This is not funny, Goldie,' she scolded, as the colt trotted happily behind her, licking the last traces of juice from his lips. 'If you do it again, you'll have to be locked up *all day*. Then we'll see how chirpy you are.'

When she arrived home, Barry was in the yard, fitting extra rails and padlocks to the shelter.

'I can't believe how smart this horse is, Shara. When he's not doing circus tricks, he's being an electrician.' He pointed to the tree that hung over the yard. 'He snapped an overhead branch so that it fell on the electric wire and shorted out the circuit!'

'Surely he didn't do that on purpose. It must have been ... a possum ... or something?'

'And we just had two more phone calls about him. Anna Paget said he opened one of her gates and let all her goats out. Wes Jenkins said he's been in their yard pulling all the washing off the line. When they chased him, he jumped over the fence and ran away.' He shook his head. 'He'll just have to stay locked up while we're not home.'

Shara groaned and ran her hand over Goldie's neck. 'What are we going to do with you, little fella? You're just too clever for your own good.'

Goldie looked back at her with large, dark eyes and pressed his head into her chest. Shara gave his forehead a rub. 'We need to have you gelded, little man. That'll keep you out of mischief.'

'I've already rung the RSPCA about that,' said Barry, packing up his tools. 'They said they can't geld him until they know who owns him.'

Shara's heart sank. 'So meanwhile he has to stay padlocked in a stable.'

'Yes, and they said there was nothing they could do for the moment. As long as he's fed properly and taken out once a day for exercise, he'll be okay.'

'Poor Goldie, he'll go crazy. He's too smart to be staring at four walls all day. He's not like normal horses.'

Shara led Goldie into the shelter next to the yard and turned him about. It was much smaller than a regular stable. Her dad had originally built it as a little feed and tack shed. Goldie would barely be able to move in it. She unclipped him and reached for the tin bucket in the corner. 'Better keep this out of reach, hey.' She padlocked the door behind her and turned to give him one last look. 'It's gonna be a long day for you, fella.'

As Shara mounted Rocko and headed out for a ride, she tried to ignore Goldie's long, pleading whinny. She kicked Rocko into a gallop and rode until she couldn't hear it anymore.

A well-worn track wove through the trees and yellowed leaves spun silently to the ground below. As she rode along the river's edge, whipbirds sent long, cracking calls to each other, and golden whistlers flitted about in the lower bushes making happy *chewitt* noises. The cool, shady stretches beneath the coachwood trees soothed away the worry in Shara's mind. She rode in and out of the riverbed, cantering along grassy stretches and then ducking to take the next crossing before reaching the old drovers' yards.

Jess's unmistakable laughter rang through the trees. She only ever laughed like that when she was with Luke. Before long a tall black horse splashed through the creek, two huge dogs gambolling alongside. Luke, with his wild hair, jeans and bare feet, rode Legsy bareback. Jess sat behind him in shorts and old runners. 'Hey, Sharsy!'

Shara sighed at the sight of them. They were such a cute couple. It would be great to find a guy like that. But right now she was having trouble even dealing with a horse. Adding a boy to her life would make things way too complicated.

Then another black horse identical to Luke's emerged from the trees. Its rider was deeply tanned and wore black jeans and a polo shirt. 'Tom!' Shara cried in surprise. 'You're home too!' She rode over and stroked Nosey's beautiful black face.

Tom grinned. 'How's vet school?'

'Great. How's your school?' Tom also went to boarding school, but his was only a couple of hours away in Brisbane. He got to be home on weekends. Over the holidays, though, he just stayed at Harry's place with Luke. His parents, both lawyers, worked non-stop.

Tom shrugged. 'I'd rather stay in Coachwood Crossing, but them's the breaks.'

'Mr Hickling came into the bakery this morning – he told me about Goldie eating all his lychees,' said Jess as they splashed through the water. 'Wasn't real impressed.'

Shara was shocked that news about the colt's antics had got out so quickly. It couldn't have been much more than an hour since she'd caught Goldie in the lychee orchard.

'The whole town is talking about him,' said Jess. 'Anna Paget was too.'

Shara groaned. 'Maybe he's just more trouble than he's worth.'

'Don't give up on him yet. He's a beautiful horse.'

They turned away from the drovers' yard and continued up along the creek through the dappled light.

'That horse has the bloodlines to be something really

special,' Luke said. 'That black stallion of the Connemans' is a smart horse, and the mare is a tablelands brumby. She'd be super hardy.'

'Yeah, well, we don't really know if they're Goldie's parents,' said Shara, feeling suddenly disheartened. 'He might just be some rogue horse.'

'Don't get down about him, Sharsy,' said Jess. 'He's just never been given a chance. With the right training and good care, he'll be fine.'

'Easy for you to say.'

'Hey, I saw those contractors at the Brisbane Ekka a few days ago,' said Tom. 'I was checking out a cattle show and they were there setting up for the Queensland roping finals.'

'What, the Conneman brothers?' asked Shara.

'Yeah. It was definitely their truck. Had their name written all over it.'

'Did they have any horses there, or just cattle?'

'Heaps of cattle and a few rough-looking horses,' said Tom. 'They looked like brumbies.'

'Was there a red taffy?'

Tom looked thoughtful, then nodded. 'Yeah, I think there was.'

'If only we could prove that she's Goldie's mother. That would show that the Connemans are Goldie's owners and should be charged with neglect, and then the RSPCA would be free to re-home him. I could just get on with owning him and taking care of him.'

Jess flashed a scheming grin. 'Well, why don't we pay the Connemans a quick visit in Brisbane? Get the proof we need?'

When Shara rode Rocko down the driveway that afternoon, she found both parents waiting for her at the top of the steps.

'Hi, guys. What's up?' Two parents usually meant things were serious.

'I want you to come inside and have a chat,' said Barry in a stern voice. He turned and walked through the door.

When Shara followed, he motioned for her to sit down at the kitchen table. Then he stood with his back to her, looking out the window. 'I was cleaning out the feed shed today, and I found some empty spray cans in the rubbish.'

'What sort of spray cans?' Shara tried her best to stay calm and sound innocent.

'Coloured hairspray cans, the sort used on those wild horses at the rodeo.' Both parents stared at Shara with cold, unmoving faces.

'Oh, them.' Shara shrugged nonchalantly. 'Jess and I used those for a fancy dress ages ago.'

Her father was unswayed. 'Stop talking rubbish, Shara, and tell me how they really got there.'

Shara sighed. 'Okay, it was us. Me and Jess.' She saw no reason to dob in Rosie and Grace.

She watched two pairs of shoulders slump. Her mother gave an exasperated sigh.

'But those Connemans deserved it.'

Barry planted his hands on his hips, the way he always did when he was about to begin a lecture. 'You can't just go around breaking the law every time you don't like something. Laws are there for very good reasons—'

Shara interrupted before her father could get into a good flow. 'But someone had to protect those horses. Don't they deserve to be protected?'

'They *are* protected, by the law, and so are their owners. They—'

'But they don't deserve to be, Dad. The Connemans are cruel.' Shara searched desperately for an ethical argument — where was Jess when she needed her? 'Don't you think we have a moral obligation to protect the weak?' She'd heard an American activist say that on television once and it had sounded very convincing.

It didn't convince her father. 'Shara, there are many ways you can put your views across and make a stand. You can lobby, start petitions, walk around naked in a sandwich board if you like, but you cannot wilfully deface someone else's property. I can see that there was good intention in what you did, but you have to live by society's rules instead of being an annoying prankster.'

'How come when adults do these things they get called *activists* and when kids do it they just get called *pranksters*? You should have seen those poor brumbies. They were completely brutalised. But now they've been rescued, thanks to our *pranks*. Look at the state Goldie was in when we found him. Those people are no good, Dad. Even Corey Duggin says so and he's a rodeo rider!'

'That's not the point, Shara. What you've done is wrong. You're damn lucky those contractors have left town or you would've been up on charges. If you pull any more stunts like that, you'll be in serious trouble, do you hear me?'

Shara sighed. 'Yes, Dad.'

Barry glared at her. 'I need to know whether your attitude is going to change, because if it's not, that horse can go to the first home that comes his way. I'm not going to feed a herd of horses for a daughter who shows no gratitude and thinks she can just go around breaking the law.'

'I'm sorry.'

'You ought to be.'

'So, are you going to punish me?' *Because a grounding could make Jess's Brisbane plan a wee bit difficult ...*

'No. I've spoken to you and I've given you a warning. Any more illegality and the horses are gone.' He looked her dead in the eye. 'Both of them!'

9

SHARA RUMMAGED THROUGH her wardrobe. What to wear to the big smoke – hmmm, something not covered in horse hair. Jeans – no clean ones. Shirt – no clean ones. Skirt – surely she had one somewhere...

She pulled a swirly yellow skirt from the very bottom of the cupboard. Aunty Vic had given it to her for Christmas; no doubt as a subtle hint that she should be more girlish. *Ugh, hurts my eyes.* She tossed it on the floor.

After trying on several tops, she threw the lot on the bed and decided to wait for Rosie to arrive. Trying to find city-friendly clothes was too stressful to contemplate solo. How on earth did she let Jess talk her into this?

She felt a pang of guilt for lying to her parents. But, she argued to herself, what else was she to do? The issue of the colt's ownership needed to be sorted so he could be gelded and cared for properly. All they needed to do was find the taffy mare and take a teensy bit of hair from her for a sample. No illegalities required.

Rosie arrived and looked at the pile on Shara's bed with disdain. Shara's wardrobe was geared towards one thing: horses.

'Lucky I brought some civilised clothes for you to try,' Rosie said, reaching into a small duffle bag and pulling out a handful of flimsy red fabric.

'What the heck is *that*?' said Shara.

'A skirt, you know, those cute little things that show off your legs.' Rosie held up the garment and stretched it between two hands.

'I thought it was a hanky,' said Shara, aghast at the teeny-weeny size of it. Not on her nelly would she be squeezing into that thing.

'Just try it,' said Rosie. 'It has to be seen *on*.'

Shara took a step backwards and grimaced.

'Cum*maahn*!'

Shara squirmed into the little red thing and stood in front of the mirror, trying to yank it down to a decent level. 'I feel half naked.'

'Leave it up!' said Rosie. 'You look hot.'

'I look like a total rodeo floozy.'

'Exactly. You'll fit right in. Got any good tops to go with it?'

After several fittings, Rosie grudgingly approved

Shara's white T-shirt with brumbies on it, and cowboy boots.

'What jewellery are you going to wear?'

'Huh?' said Shara. 'Jewellery? You didn't tell me I had to wear jewellery!'

Her self-confidence was rapidly diminishing. In Coachwood Crossing and at school, she was Shara Wilson – champion campdrafter, up-and-coming vet, equine geneticist extraordinaire. In Brisbane she'd be some lame wannabe cowgirl who didn't even own any jewellery.

Rosie rolled her eyes and pulled a small silk purse from her handbag. It was full of earrings. She brought out a jangly pair with blue crystals and held them against Shara's ears. 'Perfect,' she said, brushing Shara's hair back. 'They match your eyes.'

Shara reluctantly took out her plain old sleepers and hooked the earrings into her earlobes.

'What about your charm bracelet?' said Rosie.

'Oh, yeah.' Shara opened the drawer in her bedside table.

The delicate silver chain bore fifteen tiny charms. Every charm marked a new year in her life; a bootie for her first birthday and a teddy bear for her second. By her fifth, it was a horseshoe and for her sixth, after falling off her first pony, a tiny helmet; the little silver horse had been for her twelfth birthday, just after she'd bought Rocko from the saleyards, and for her fourteenth a tiny book had celebrated her scholarship to Canningdale College.

Shara draped the bracelet over her wrist and held it out for Rosie to clasp. 'Make sure it's clipped on properly. I would die if I lost it.' It was one of her most treasured possessions, so treasured, in fact, that she only ever wore it for Christmas and her birthday. 'Do I look okay?' She turned around.

'What about your hair?'

'What's wrong with my hair?'

Rosie looked at the ponytail clamped to the back of Shara's head. 'You look like someone who's about to either muck out stables or play tennis.'

'We're only supposed to be going to the movies,' Shara argued.

'But it's in the *city*,' said Rosie. 'And it's that big 3D screen. One of the biggest in the southern hemisphere. I almost wish I was going myself.'

'Rosie, we're not really going to the movies, remember?'

'It doesn't matter, we still have to convince your parents that you are. Besides, you might snag yourself a cowboy at the show.'

Shara snorted. She didn't know what was worse, being coerced into this web of deceit, being forced into a skirt, or having Rosie trying to get her a love-life. 'I don't like cowboys.'

She scruffed her hair. 'What *will* I do with my hair, then? It's so boring.'

'It's not, it's gorgeous,' said Rosie, running her fingers through it and looking at Shara in the mirror. 'It's so thick and *blonde*. Wish I had hair like that.' Then she pulled a petulant face. 'Tom might even notice that I exist!'

'Oh, Rosie, you two are total besties.'

Rosie flicked her wispy hair over her shoulder and pouted. 'I want to be more than just besties.'

'Maybe he's just shy.'

'Maybe.' Rosie took Shara by the shoulders and planted her firmly into a chair in front of the mirror. Shara sat obediently while Rosie plucked and preened and forced her hair into an amazing side-part do, talking the whole time about Tom. She applied make-up and a squirt of something floral-smelling. By the time she was finished, Shara had to admit the results were good. She twirled in front of the mirror, admiring the new girly version of herself. 'I should do this more often.'

She picked up her denim jacket, and stuffed both her wallet and keys into the pocket. 'Come on. Luke'll be waiting.'

Outside, Barry had Luke pinned to the side of his HQ ute, giving him a stiff lecture on speed limits and passenger safety.

'Not a problem, Baz,' Luke said cheerfully.

Shara saw her father's jaw tighten. He hated being called 'Baz'. He ran his eyes over Luke's old yellow ute, with its dark-blue door from a wrecker's yard. 'You're to give me a call straight away if you have any engine troubles.'

'Yes, sir,' said Luke. 'It shouldn't be a problem, though. This old girl will get us down and back in one piece.'

Shara gave the doorhandle a yank and slid in next to Jess. As they drove out the gate, she waved to her father, who stood on the verandah with hands on hips and a rigid face. Safely down the road, Shara turned to Jess. 'Did you bring some scissors?'

'Yep!' Jess drew a small box of clip-lock bags and a pair of hairdressing scissors from her bag. 'You bring the camera?'

Shara pulled it out of her pocket and aimed the lens back towards them. 'Lean in!'

The flash went off, leaving blotches of colour in her vision. The girls huddled over the LCD screen, admiring their exaggerated smiles.

'The scissors won't be much use,' said Luke. 'You need a hair follicle for a DNA sample. You'll have to pluck it, not cut it.'

'Cool, let's go pluck!' said Shara.

10

IT WAS DARK when they arrived in Brisbane. They found a park down the road from the showgrounds. A bustle of cars, trucks and taxis tore past in streams of red and white light.

'Come on, Shara,' said Jess, grabbing her hand and leaping into the traffic.

'Holy crap,' said Shara, stumbling off the kerb.

They crossed three lanes and waited, toes on the white lines, until another gap appeared in the rush of vehicles. A taxi zoomed behind them and honked. Shara jumped in fright and Jess pulled her forward across another three lanes and onto the footpath. Behind them, the cars slowed and the lights turned red. Luke calmly crossed at the intersection.

Jess took Shara by one arm and Luke by the other, and linked together, they headed for the showgrounds. Before they reached the main gates they could hear the country music, crooning cattle and over-excited commentators, all sounding totally out of whack with the roar of city traffic.

At the back of the main arena was a cluster of trucks and horse floats, four-wheel drives and dust-covered vehicles. Beyond that, Shara could see caravans and temporary accommodation. They bought tickets and strolled through the turnstiles into the smell of popcorn, horse hair and sickly-sweet fairy floss.

In the arena the Clydesdale tug-o-war was on, with at least sixty kids braced against a long rope, chattering excitedly. The rope was attached to the harness of two huge feather-legged horses with muscled hindquarters. The announcer bellowed to the handler to take up the slack. 'Averaging twenty-five kilos per kid, that there is a tonne and a half of kids!'

'My money's on the Clydies,' said Luke.

'No way, they'll let the kids win,' said Jess.

Shara thought it looked evenly matched and couldn't decide either way.

They stayed and watched three rounds of squealing children being dragged through the dirt, pulling and laughing and eventually conceding before the wild goat race was announced as the next event.

'Shoulda brought your coloured hairspray,' said Luke, and Jess punched him on the shoulder.

They left the main arena and mingled with the crowds. There were trade booths filled with sumptuous leather horse gear and country clothing. Agricultural advisors had information tables, and produce companies spruiked their products. The friends strolled between rides and showbag stalls until they came to a line of bunting flags fencing them off from the trucks and the animals. Men in black T-shirts stood, arms folded, at intervals along the barrier.

Shara scanned the surrounds. 'How are we going to get out the back?'

'Let's come in from that park behind,' said Luke. 'Maybe we can find a section that they've left unguarded.'

They slipped out of the arena perimeters and through some empty pavilions. The showgrounds were immense and the roping finals only filled a small corner of them. As they left the brightly lit commotion behind, trucks and vans formed strange shapes in the darkness, with the occasional human silhouette moving between them. It became quiet and creepy.

'You guys stay here while I try to find somewhere to get in,' said Luke, staring up at the two-metre cyclone wire fence that stood between them and the competitors' area.

'How about we check up this way?' Shara pointed in the opposite direction.

'Okay, meet you back here in ten minutes.' Luke

slipped through some shrubs and darted off towards the back of the arena.

Jess and Shara continued along the fence in the direction of a block of stables.

'Look through there!' said Jess, stopping outside the huge open doorway. 'There's nothing to stop us walking straight through and out into the competitors' area.'

Shara stared in at the horses tied in the aisle and the riders sitting on buckets cleaning bridles. Jess was right; there was no barrier at all. She looked down at her red skirt and wished she'd worn her old riding jeans. 'I'm not exactly dressed like a competitor. I'll stand out like stallions' balls.'

'Won't matter if we're quick.'

'Should we go and get Luke?'

Jess looked at her watch. 'He won't be back yet. Let's just have a quick squiz before we meet up with him.'

They walked directly through the stable block, heads high, as if they owned the place. No one seemed to take much notice of them – they just carried on with brushing and watering and feeding horses.

'Now where?' said Shara as they exited the rear of the building.

'This way,' said Jess.

Shara followed her across a small exercise arena and continued through dimly lit rows of vehicles, listening to the muffled voices and clinking of cutlery and plates from inside the caravans.

'Let's keep it low-key,' Jess breathed. 'If we get busted out here without a pass, we'll get kicked out and then we'll never get the hair sample.'

'Is that the Connemans' truck?' Shara pointed to the outer rim of the car park, where the top of a semitrailer with livestock crates on the back loomed above the smaller trucks.

'Sure looks like it,' said Jess. 'Let's go!'

'Oh, God,' groaned Shara, uncertainty hitting her like a wave of cement. 'I really don't know if we should be doing this.'

'Bit late now,' said Jess, and before Shara could voice any more doubts, she was being led through a dark labyrinth of trailers.

'Shara?'

Shara froze. That was Corey's voice! He walked towards them in his big black hat and a burgundy red shirt with a roping saddle and a tangle of leather straps in his arms.

'Hi!' Shara plastered on a huge, nervous smile. 'What are *you* doing here?'

He gave her a shrewd look. 'What are *you* doing here?'

'Just came to watch some roping,' Jess interjected.

Corey addressed Shara. 'Thought you didn't like rodeo.'

89

'Roping's okay,' she shrugged.

'This is the competitors' area. You riding here?'

'We're visiting a friend,' said Jess quickly.

Corey stayed focused on Shara. His eyes seemed to go right through her and make the truth impossible to hide. 'Are you visiting the Connemans?'

'No! No... of course not. We didn't even know they were here.' Shara's voice was a squeaky stammer. She was *so* lying and it was *so* obvious. She could almost hear Jess's groan at her complete inability to keep it together.

'They're not the sort of people you want to mess with.'

'Why would we want to mess with them?' said Jess, taking Shara by the arm again. 'We have to go, or we'll miss the finals.'

'They're not on for another hour,' said Shara.

'We have to go anyway.' Jess hauled her away until they were behind a big, stinking rubbish hopper, then spun around to face her. 'Oh my God, you've totally got the hots for that rodeo schmuck. You were about to tell him everything!'

'What, are you nuts?' Shara pulled a face. 'I was just surprised to see him, that's all. It caught me off-guard.'

'Crap!' said her friend with an appalled laugh. 'You never smile at *me* like that.'

'Well, you're not six foot tall with a purebred quarter horse underneath you,' said Shara.

Jess snorted in disgust. 'He is a total player. Pull yourself together before I slap you!'

Shara rolled her eyes. 'Let's just go.'

Jess was like a ferret in a rabbit warren, weaving in and out between vans and trucks. Shara could hardly keep up with her. It wasn't long before they realised that there were very few dark places to hide. They zigzagged from shadow to shadow, finding very little cover. If someone was to walk out of their van, they'd be caught, frozen under a porch light with nowhere to run. A dog barked and threw itself at the inside wall of a truck, snarling. Shara jumped backwards.

Two arms caught her and a hand clamped over her mouth. She felt her stomach knot as she was dragged slowly backwards, one step at a time, silently, into a dark space. She could only watch as, up ahead, Jess slipped silently behind a horse truck and disappeared.

'Sshh,' her assailant whispered into her ear.

From inside the truck, a man's voice growled. 'Lie down!' There was a yelp and then quiet.

Shara didn't dare breathe. The dog let out a low, *I-know-you're-still-out-there* growl and then yelped as its owner kicked it again.

'What are you doing back here?' It was Corey. Shara winced as she was spun around. 'What are you and your mate up to? You're not going to ruin the nationals for everyone with some stupid protest, are you?' His voice was like a sharp pinch.

'No, we just . . .' How on earth could she explain? She couldn't, she realised – she might as well come clean. 'We just want to find Goldie's mother,' she said. 'So we can prove who owns him. We're not—'

'You don't know who you're messing with,' he hissed, and it left her wondering whether he included himself in that category or whether he was just talking about the Connemans.

'I'm sorry . . .'

He pointed his thumb back towards the stable. 'Get out of here before you get busted. Just go home. The animal shelter will sort out who owns that horse.'

'They can't, not without proof. We just need a DNA sample. A bit of hair, that's all. Then we'll go, I promise. Oh, and a photo.'

She heard Corey exhale.

'Jess is . . . I have to catch up with her. She's . . .' Shara pointed to where she had last seen Jess. Damn, now she had lost her, and by now Luke would be waiting for them.

Corey followed her eyes. There was a charged silence.

'Please?' she whispered.

He looked down at her with a searching face, then somehow his hand found hers. 'I'll help you find her. Follow me. You'll be okay if you're with a competitor.'

He led her calmly through the maze of trucks with her hand squeezed tightly in his. Shara followed obediently until she saw a large red semitrailer parked by some cattle yards in the distance. 'That's their truck,' she whispered.

Before Corey could answer, a tall, wiry figure emerged from behind the big semi and walked towards them, with a cigarette smouldering between his lips. Shara felt her heart beat out of whack. Her throat tightened. Corey dropped her hand and kept walking without changing rhythm and she forced her feet to continue alongside him.

Corey nodded as he passed the man. 'Graham.'

Graham Conneman grunted and a trail of cigarette smoke and BO lingered after him. Corey took Shara's hand again and squeezed it even tighter, as though issuing a warning. Uncertainty beat through her veins. What was she getting herself into? She really didn't know Corey well. Jess was right, he was a player and everyone knew it and now he had her hand in a vice-like grip in some dark alley in Brisbane.

Two large men approached them. Corey pulled Shara to a stop near a long gooseneck trailer and stepped around in front of her to push her against the wall of the truck. He put his face as close as possible to hers without touching, obscuring her view. 'Don't move,' he murmured, and she felt his breath on her neck. 'They're security guards. Just play along.' His nose touched her softly beneath her ear, making tingles shoot up her spine. 'Sorry,' he whispered. Then to her alarm, she felt his leg rub against hers.

'You got wristbands, kids?' said one of the men as they got closer.

Corey put one arm around Shara's shoulder and held the other up, revealing a paper bracelet with a barcode on it. 'Competitor, mate.' Shara looked away, thinking she might die of embarrassment.

'Take that somewhere else, hey?' said the other man, running his eyes over Shara, and to her relief, they kept walking.

She let Corey's hand rest on her waist as he walked her away. His stride was still filled with self-assurance. Jess was right, he was a total sleaze. When she could no longer hear the guards' footsteps, she shoved him off and as she did, her charm bracelet caught on his shirt. 'What the hell was that?' she said angrily as she tugged at her bracelet. It wouldn't come free.

He stared down at her. 'I was saving your arse. Don't bother thanking me.'

She glared at him and pulled at his shirt. 'What for?'

He put his hands over hers and stopped her tugging. 'There are rodeo groupies out the back all the time, chasing the cowboys. They never worry about it,' he said as he took her wrist in his hand and felt for the bracelet. 'They'd have kicked you out otherwise.'

'Yeah, well, that's *not* why I'm here,' she reminded him curtly.

'I know,' he chuckled. 'Sorry, I didn't mean to ... you know ...' He burst out laughing.

Shara was incensed. Was the thought of really kissing her so hilarious to him? She turned on her heel to find Jess.

'Hey, you got yourself into this,' he reminded her.

She was about to turn back and give him an earful, but a gentle and unmistakable snort in the back of the red truck made her stop. 'That was a horse!'

There it was again: a long, blubbery exhalation; the stamp of a hoof; the dull *thud-thud-thud* of poo hitting timber floorboards.

'It's inside the Connemans' truck.' Shara heard shuffling, chomping, chewing, tearing at hay, familiar sounds that filled her with confidence. She hoped like anything it was the red taffy mare so she could just get her hair sample and get out of there.

'It'll be the mare you're looking for,' said Corey, as though reading her mind. 'They keep her as a spare for the wild horse race because she's a brumby. Even though she's been in captivity for years, she's still pretty flighty.'

'Yeah, well, no wonder, if they brutalise her all the time,' snapped Shara.

'Want some help?'

'I'm sure I'll be fine, thank you.'

'Oh, come on,' he said in a softer voice. 'I'm sorry. I shouldn't have laughed at you back there. Let me help you. She can be a real handful, that mare.' He gave her a smile that she still found smirky and arrogant, but kind of cute at the same time.

'Oh, all right!' she said grudgingly. 'But don't go grabbing me again, okay? I'm not into cowboys.'

11

SHARA WAS RELIEVED to find Jess already hanging off the side of the semitrailer when they got to it. Jess looked taken aback when Corey appeared, but Shara put her finger to her lips and mimed *It's okay*.

Jess pointed into the back of the crate. 'I think we found her!'

Shara raised a foot onto the bar and hoisted herself up against the side of the truck. She peered in through a barred window. Two red eyes glowed back.

Corey hopped up beside her. 'Is it the mare?'

'I don't know. I can't see.' She squinted into the black void. Corey pulled out his phone and woke up the screen, then held it up to face the window. In the faint light it shed, Shara could just make out the mare's pale mane. 'That's her!'

'We'll have to get her to come closer so we can grab a piece of hair,' whispered Jess.

But the mare was cross-tied, a rope from either side of the truck holding her in the centre of the vehicle. 'See if you can reach her tail,' Shara whispered back.

'Move over.' Corey pulled out a pocket knife and reached in through the small window. He hacked at the lead rope until it gave way, falling below the mare's chin.

Shara let herself down and went around to the other side of the truck. Jess followed. 'What's *he* doing here?' she hissed when they were out of earshot.

'He's stalking me. Let's just get the hair and get out! Luke will be waiting for us!'

'I sent him a message telling him how to get in,' whispered Jess.

They climbed up and peered in. Jess pulled gently at the rope, bringing the mare's head towards the window. The horse snorted in fear. Shara reached through the bars and, with a quick tug, plucked a strand of the mare's forelock. 'Got it!'

The mare threw her head in the air and jumped backwards. Shara lost her footing and fell, banging her elbow on the way down and landing awkwardly on one knee. She writhed on the ground and silently cursed.

'You okay?' Corey appeared beside her and crouched down on one heel, snickering.

'It's not funny,' she hissed.

He chuckled and held out a hand to help her up.

Shara slapped it away and pulled herself upright. 'Sadist.'

'We need a photo,' whispered Jess, who still hung from the side of the truck.

'Don't worry about me, I'll be fine,' grumbled Shara sarcastically.

'Where's your camera?' asked Corey. 'I'll get the photo.' He took the camera from her and hopped up onto the truck again.

A light came on in a caravan nearby, and Shara could hear a person moving about inside. A door swung open and she watched in horror as a wiry figure stood silhouetted against the yellow light. *'Guys!'* she hissed.

The camera flashed and there was an explosion of drumming hooves inside the truck. Shara heard the mare's head smash against the roof. Corey leapt down from the window and promptly tripped over Shara, landing heavily beside her. She heard him stifle a laugh.

'HEY!' a voice shouted. 'Someone's stealing my horse!'

There was a screaming whinny, then shouting, lights snapping on, more lights, voices everywhere.

'Oh, *crap*,' said Corey, his tone instantly changing. 'It's Mark Conneman. Shara, get up and let's get out of here.' He put both hands under her arms and helped her scramble to her feet.

'Quick, Sharsy!' said Jess, as she sprinted past.

'Call security,' a voice yelled.

'Stop them!' shouted another.

Blind panic overrode the burning pain that shot through Shara's knee at every step as she was dragged along behind Corey. People appeared from everywhere, dim silhouettes in the dark, until suddenly they were blocking the path. Corey stopped. He dropped her hand. They both stepped slowly backwards as they became encircled.

A hand grabbed the back of Shara's neck and she pulled her head into her shoulders, gasping. The stench of stale cigarette smoke hung all around her.

'Let her go,' said Corey, spinning around. He looked at the person who gripped her by the neck, and held both hands up. 'We were just mucking about, Graham – we didn't mean anything, just let her go.'

'What do you want with my horse?'

'Nothing, Graham, honestly.'

Shara clawed at the fingers gripping her neck. They were getting tighter. She could feel the blood pumping in her ears.

'They've cut its lead rope.' Mark Conneman appeared from nowhere. He ran his eyes over Shara. 'Who's she?'

'Just a friend.' Corey kept stepping towards her, his eyes flashing from one brother to the other. Something about his face filled Shara with dread. She squeezed her eyes closed and tried to breathe.

'She's trouble,' said the voice behind the steely fingers.

People who had come out to look began backing away and disappearing, as though something was going to happen that they didn't want to witness.

'She's with me, Graham.' Corey kept moving closer. 'Don't hurt her.'

The grip on Shara's neck loosened ever so slightly and she took her chance. She struggled violently and made a dash for freedom, but felt her arm nearly pull out of its socket as she was grabbed again. 'Where are you going, you little tart?'

Corey burst forward with a flying fist. It was so fast she didn't see it connect, but she heard a sickening crunch and the grip on her arm released.

Shara pitched backwards, arms flailing. 'Corey,' she screamed. *'Behind you!'*

As if in slow motion, Corey turned to face the other Conneman, who swung his fist across Corey's jaw like a wrecking ball. Corey's head jerked backwards. He twisted and lurched, landing facedown on the ground with a thud.

Shara's scream was beyond her control. It tore through the darkness. Then the world went crazy around her.

'Cops!' someone yelled, and the word seemed to make

people scatter. The crowd changed. Some faces dissolved, and new ones appeared: good faces, concerned faces. They ran to Corey, who lay motionless on the ground. Shara followed them and knelt beside him. 'Corey?'

Nothing.

'What happened?' Luke panted.

'We got busted.'

Luke rolled him over. 'Corey, can you hear me?'

A groan gurgled from Corey's throat.

'He needs an ambulance.'

'Someone get St John's out here,' said a stranger.

Shara brushed the thick dark hair back from Corey's forehead. He groaned again. *'Corey?'*

Luke illuminated his phone screen and held it to Corey's face. Corey's eyes were closed and he drew short raspy breaths. 'It's okay, mate,' said Luke. 'Hang in there.'

Tears streamed down Shara's face. This wasn't meant to happen. Everything was going wrong. She bent forward. 'Please be okay, Corey,' she whispered.

The next two hours were a blur. There were flashing lights and people in uniforms with a stretcher. There was the inside of the ambulance and two people leaning over Corey and speaking calmly to him. Then there were police. Jess and Luke were in the back of one of their cars.

Shara couldn't remember how she came to sit alone in a dingy, fluorescent-lit waiting room at a police station for hours. Someone passed her a phone, and she could hear her father's voice at the other end, but all she could do was cry. No one would tell her what was going on. More police were hovering around and Shara could have sworn she saw someone she vaguely recognised talking to them. Eventually her mother and father arrived and shot anxious questions at her faster than she could answer. Later, she fell asleep against her father's shoulder. When she woke, he was standing at a counter filling out forms. The next thing she knew, she was being tucked into bed.

'Is Corey going to be okay?'

'Sshh, just go to sleep now, honey. We'll talk in the morning.'

12

THE TENSION IN the house the next morning was excruciating. No one spoke. Her father made slow, deliberate movements around the kitchen while her mother sat at the table with her arms folded. One minute Shara was sitting still, chewing slowly, uncertainly, on her toast, and the next her father exploded.

'What the *heck* is going on, Shara? Do you have *any* idea what it is like to be rung up by the police at ten o'clock at night and told that your daughter is in Brisbane at a police station? Why on earth were you trying to steal a horse?'

'We weren't trying to steal it, we just—'

'Oh, come *on*!' said Louise. 'They found a pocket knife in the truck with Corey Duggin's name on it, for God's sake. You had that horse's halter half off. How else did that Duggin boy get kicked by a horse?'

'What? What did you say?' said Shara, incredulous.

Her head throbbed. 'Corey didn't get kicked by a horse. He—'

'Enough of your lies,' her father bellowed. 'That kid is trouble, Shara. I don't care if he's John Duggin's boy. I don't want you anywhere near him.'

'But, you've got to believe me. He was—'

'Believe you? After that story about the 3D movie you could only see in Brisbane? You have *got* to be joking! I don't want to hear another word from you. I can't stand the lies.'

'Dad, they . . .' Shara tried desperately to get her story out but it fell on deaf ears. She looked at her mum and burst into tears. 'You guys don't even care what the truth is!'

She knew she had chosen the wrong words before they even left her mouth. Her father thumped his fist on the kitchen bench so hard that the apples jumped about in the fruit bowl.

'Don't care? How *dare* you?' he roared. 'We give you everything. We drive two hours to Brisbane and sit in a police station all night. We let you bring home a rogue colt, which, by the way, will be on a truck back to the shelter this afternoon, and *we* don't care?'

'Corey was looking after me, Dad.' It was true. He had done everything he could to keep her out of trouble. Everything was all wrong.

'Save it for the police, Shara,' said Louise. 'They'll be here at nine.' She got up and left the room. Barry followed, slamming the door after him.

At five to nine Shara was sitting in the lounge room next to her mother, frozen, staring at the frayed edges of the Persian rug. The washing machine hummed through the floorboards. A thick blanket of sadness suffocated her, sapping her energy.

Barry showed a police officer through the door. It wasn't Sergeant Bigwood. This man was middle-aged, stocky, with greying hair. Behind him was a woman, about the same age. Both had grave expressions on their faces.

Louise motioned for them to sit down. The policeman pulled out a notepad and began taking notes, asking for Shara's full name and various other details. Then he asked her what happened. He listened silently as Shara spoke in a monotone until she got to the part where Corey was hurt in the fight, and started crying again.

Then it was the female officer's turn. She talked to Shara about breaking and entering, and outlined the problems with vigilante justice. She described the juvenile justice system, criminal records and anything else she could think of to thoroughly put the wind up not just Shara, but her parents as well. She wasn't unpleasant. She wasn't heavy. She sounded more like a school counsellor than a police officer. Everything she said was true and, worse, it made sense. As she spoke, Shara kept her eyes fixed firmly on the fraying rug. The washing machine reached spin cycle and the floor vibrated even faster.

Her parents said nothing through the whole interview. They didn't stick up for her at all.

When the police finally left she managed to escape to her room, where she sat in a daze of confused and whirling thoughts. How had Jess and Luke got home last night? Were they okay? Was Corey okay? There would be no point sending Jess a text or trying to ring her. Her parents would have confiscated her phone for sure – it was always the first thing to go when she got in trouble. Instead, Shara sent Luke a text message, asking if he had heard any news about Corey.

Outside she heard her father's four-wheel drive back up to the horse float and moments later the sounds of hooves up a tailgate. Shara rushed to the window and saw Rocko's big brown rump move up into the float and take its place next to Goldie's.

'Oh my God, no!'

A sense of absolute panic overwhelmed her. She threw her phone aside, raced out the door and ran down the hallway as if her life depended on it, screaming, 'Dad! Dad! No!' She hurled herself down the back steps, sobbing. 'I'm sorry!'

Her father clinched the handles on the tailgate without looking at her. He walked to the car, opened the door and got in. The engine started and the float rolled down the driveway.

For a brief moment the world took on perfect clarity. She registered the breeze on her face; the sound of distant bird calls and a passenger train rumbling along somewhere lower in the valley; everything was as it should be. And then her voice ripped through the middle of it all, begging and sobbing as she stood in the driveway, hands over her face. She felt her mother's arm around her.

'Where's he taken them, Mum? Please ask him to bring them back. Please, Mum.'

Her mother spoke gently but firmly. 'Goldie's going back to the animal shelter, and your father's taking Rocko out to Blakely Downs.'

'Blakely Downs!' choked Shara. Blakely Downs was a huge cattle station more than ten hours' drive away. 'That's fifty thousand hectares! I'll never see him again!'

'Your father warned you, Shara.' Her mum's voice was cold.

'They'll give Goldie back to the rodeo.'

Her mum said nothing.

'I didn't even get to say goodbye. He didn't let me say goodbye.'

The rest of the morning was just one long, miserable stretch of time. Shara lay curled in a ball on her bed. How had her life become so messed up so quickly?

The vision of the two horses disappearing in the float wouldn't leave her mind. It was as though she had to keep replaying it over and over for her to be able to believe, comprehend, that they were actually gone from her life, especially Rocko, whom she had spent so many years rehabilitating. The sound of their hooves walking up the ramp into the float kept ringing in her ears.

Then the yelling and the flashing lights from the previous night cut across her thoughts. She shuddered as she felt the cruel grip on the back of her neck again.

And Corey; his teasing laughter at the truck, but then the way he had fought for her, literally. She remembered that horrible crunching sound and winced. Was he *okay*? No one had told her anything; they were all too busy yelling at her.

From her floordrobe of dirty jeans and shirts, her phone let out a muffled jingle. A pang of hope jolted her off the bed and she rummaged desperately and fruitlessly for it through the mess on the floor. Finally, a buzzing voicemail tone helped her locate it.

'Shara, it's Luke. Corey's still in hospital. Can you meet me at my place this arvo? It's really important.'

Shara filled with dread. Why would Luke ring instead of text? Why did he need to meet her? Had something really bad happened to Corey? Was Jess grounded? So many questions. She thrust her feet into her boots and threw on a jumper. Nobody had said anything about her being grounded.

13

A MAN IN a crisp white shirt and a dark blue tie was sitting on Luke's couch, a mug of coffee in front of him. He looked weirdly out of place in Luke's tiny flat, which was a converted stable full of second-hand furniture. Luke was sitting on a stool with his elbows on the kitchenette bench, his face down and his hands clasped over his head. He didn't look up as Shara peered through the split doors.

'You must be Shara,' the man said, standing up as she walked in.

He was fiftyish and handsome in an old kind of way, with tanned skin and brilliant white teeth. She recognised him as the man at the police station. Tom's dad. A lawyer. Something about the sight of him made her want to turn and walk straight out the door again. *This was bad. Really bad.* She tried to think of an excuse to leave but couldn't.

Tom's dad extended his hand to her over the cable reel that Luke used as a coffee table. 'Ian Hoskins.'

Shara took his smooth, cool hand, shook it and saw his expression become formal and businesslike. He gestured to the chair in front of him. 'Would you like a cup of anything?'

She shook her head and sat where she was told.

'Tell me the truth, Shara. Did you kids have any notions at all about trying to steal that horse?'

She didn't answer. The question made her angry. His being a lawyer didn't mean she had to tell him anything.

'Shara, I'm trying to help Corey,' he eventually said. 'I just need to hear your version of events.'

'Why? He's got his own dad.'

'Yes, John's a good friend of mine,' said Mr Hoskins coldly, 'and right now he's at the hospital with his injured son. He's asked for my help.'

'Ian's okay, Shara. He's . . . helped me out before.' Luke's voice was flat.

Shara looked from Luke to Mr Hoskins. She was faintly aware that Luke already had a history with the police. This would be the last thing he needed.

'Is Corey okay?'

'There've been a few complications,' said Mr Hoskins.

'Like what?'

'Dislocated jaw, for a start. Broken knuckles.' Mr Hoskins' voice became disapproving. 'Concussion. They need to make sure there's no swelling around his brain before they discharge him. The police also want to talk to him. The Conneman brothers intend to lay charges.'

Shara couldn't believe what she was hearing. Corey had nothing to do with this. None of this was his idea. He'd become involved only as a way of looking out for her. She looked to Luke. 'And Jess?'

'The police have been to her place too.' Luke's voice was empty. 'Her dad rang me. She's not allowed to see me for six weeks.' He put his head down on the bench in front of him.

'Six weeks?'

'I should have talked her out of it. I shouldn't have let her go through with it.'

'This wasn't *your* fault, Luke.'

'I'm the one who drove her down there.'

'Luke's right. None of you should have gone down there in the first place,' said Mr Hoskins.

'Yeah, well, easy to say that now,' snapped Shara. God, adults were so good at stating the bleeding obvious. 'That horse was locked inside a truck – there was absolutely no way we were going to steal it! All we wanted was a photo and a lock of hair.'

'What for?'

'Because if we could prove that the Conneman brothers owned the colt . . .'

'What colt?'

'Goldie. He turned up in Coachwood Crossing after they left town, badly malnutritioned and—'

'Malnourished.'

'He was starving, okay?' Shara could hear her voice rising. 'If we could prove the Connemans owned the colt and neglected him, then he could be seized by the RSPCA. They could re-home him and make sure he was properly cared for.'

'Re-homed to *you*,' Mr Hoskins clarified.

Shara glared at him. What did that have to do with anything? Whose side was this guy on?

'It's unlikely that the authorities would take the Connemans' animals if they use them to earn a living,' continued Mr Hoskins. 'That's why there are still elephants in circuses. It's why brumbies can be used in rodeos. They might be closely monitored by animal welfare groups, but they're rarely removed. But what's the colt got to do with the mare you were . . . plucking?'

Shara went through the whole story again — her silver taffy theory; the little brumby mare and the black stallion; the idea that the mare was the colt's mother. If they could prove the parentage, they'd prove Goldie had been owned — and maltreated — by the Connemans. She recounted the events of the previous evening and Corey's attempts to protect her.

Mr Hoskins listened patiently while she spewed it

all out. Then he stood, walked around to her side of the coffee table and put his hand on her shoulder. 'I'll see what I can do to help Corey.'

Luke stood up and fumbled with something around his neck. 'Shara, if you see Jess, can you give her this? Tell her I'll get it back from her in six weeks.' He handed her a smooth stone pendant on a thin leather strap, his face intense. 'Tell her I'll be back.'

'Where are you going?'

'Blakely Downs,' he said in an empty voice. 'No point staying around here.'

Shara's heart ached for Jess. She'd be shattered. Everyone was shattered. What had they gone and done? She took the stone from Luke, putting it carefully inside her top pocket and buttoning it closed. 'I'll get it to her somehow.' Then she watched as he followed Mr Hoskins out the door.

She just wanted everything to go back to how it was before that stupid trip to Brisbane. She wanted Corey out of hospital and back on his big quarter horse. She wanted her father to come home and smack her playfully on the side of the head with the newspaper. She wanted her Rocko back.

And what would become of Goldie? She'd let herself dream that one day he would be hers – but now she'd well and truly blown any chance of that.

14

'YOUR FATHER RANG to say both horses are settled,' said Louise from the kitchen sink. She pulled off her rubber gloves and reached for a tea towel. 'Rocko got to Blakely Downs okay.'

Shara took a seat at the table, unable to contemplate breakfast. 'He'll have to . . .' She closed her mouth tightly, as the pain of talking about him caught her throat. 'He'll have to take Rocko's shoes off before he turns him out.'

'One of the ringers has already done it.'

Shara sucked in a breath, silently hating someone else for taking charge of her horse, even if they were doing the right thing. 'Is Goldie back at the shelter?'

'He's at the vet hospital, waiting for ownership to be sorted out so he can be gelded.'

Shara got up, walked back to her room and closed the door. She tidied her desk and pulled a balled-up T-shirt from under the bed. If she kept busy she might not feel so much like smashing something. She bundled up her dirty clothes from the floor and carried them to the laundry.

As she threw her denim jacket into the machine, something clunked. She pulled it back out, checked the pockets and found her camera. She leaned against the washing machine as she scrolled through the photos.

Shara and Jess in the front of the car with cheek-splitting toothy grins > Jess and Luke on the street corner in Brisbane > The mare, head high, eyes rolling.

Shara stared a little closer, then panned in to a black smudge on the horse's shoulder. Was that a scar – or a *brand*? She squinted long and hard at it.

B... 2... B... She gasped. 'Bred to Buck!'

She hurried back to her room and drummed her fingers on her desk as her computer gurgled to life. She poked the memory card into it and the photos came up on screen. Yep – that was a brand, all right. Now, what had she done with that hair sample?

'Oh, crap!' She ran back to the laundry, fished her jacket out of the machine and rummaged through the pockets for the lock of the taffy's mane. 'Gotcha!' she said, and carried it back down the hallway in its little clip-lock bag.

She carefully saved the photo of the mare onto a thumb drive. As she searched for the cap in her jewellery box, she was momentarily distracted by her charm bracelet lying on the cushion of blue velvet. Something about it wasn't quite right. She pulled the bracelet out and jangled it, looking over the charms.

A link was broken and the little silver horse, the one that represented Rocko, was missing. Shara stared at the broken bracelet. The charm must have come off when it got stuck on Corey's shirt. She thought of him leaning close to her, against the truck . . . She closed her eyes and remembered how his breath had felt against her neck.

Then she shook herself. She'd be lucky if Corey ever spoke to her again.

She placed the hair sample into a small jewellery purse, together with the thumb drive, and zipped it safely into the front pouch of her backpack.

Not only were these the key to Goldie's identity and a chance to help him, but they would confirm that the Connemans were lying, dodgy, cruel scumbags. If she could prove that, she might have some hope of persuading her parents to return her horses.

Hex greeted her on the front verandah. 'Hey, fella,' she said softly. She pulled a three-day-old ham sandwich out of her bag and held it in the air, making him stretch his neck and hold his head high. 'Are you a good boy?' she asked in her special training tone.

Hex nodded his head, lifted a paw and whined. Shara ripped off a portion of the sandwich and threw it to him.

'And are you well?' She held another piece out and gave the signal to speak. Hex growled and woofed together. 'You miss Rocko?' She gave him another bit and held some more out. 'That's no good. What else did you say? Dad should give my horses back? Yes, I think so too. You can have *two* bits for that one.' Shara tossed Hex the rest of the sandwich, and stepped off the front verandah.

She walked purposefully along the dirt track that wove between gum trees and wattles and down the steep hill that ran along the front boundary of the property, begrudging the time it took to get anywhere without a horse to ride. She headed towards town, her thoughts weaving in crazy, confusing patterns.

As the track connected with Coachwood Road, the main way into town, she stepped out to cross and was forced back by the rushing wind of a passing car. It honked loudly.

'Whoa!'

The small red car sped away, leaving a trail of exhaust smoke behind it. As Shara stood on the side of the road, regaining her balance, the sound of a cantering horse clattered behind her.

'Coo-ee!'

'Jess!'

Her bestie pulled Dodger back to a trot and clip-clopped along the road towards her. 'What happened,

Sharsy? No one will tell me anything. Mum and Dad won't let me talk to Luke. They're so angry at him for driving us down there. They reckon I can't talk to him for six whole weeks. They even took my phone off me so he can't ring!'

'He told me.'

'When?' Jess reined her horse to a stop. 'Did you see him? What did he say?'

'He's pretty upset.' Shara fished in her top pocket. 'He wanted me to give you this.'

She watched the shock grow on her friend's face as she took the moonstone Shara held out.

'It's a promise that he'll see me again,' said Jess. She stared at Shara, bewildered. 'Where is he *going*?'

'I don't know. He just said he'd see you in six weeks,' said Shara gently. This was so messed up. Everyone's lives were being hammered. 'I'm so sorry.'

'He didn't have to leave town!' Anger grew in Jess's voice. 'My God, I can't believe my parents have driven him out of town!'

'It was his choice, Jess. He probably knew you'd still come and find him and get yourself into even more trouble.'

Jess slipped off Dodger and stood with her face hidden in the flaps of the saddle. She thumped the fender with a frustrated fist.

Shara put a hand on her shoulder and Jess looked

sideways at her. Her focus changed abruptly. 'Why are you on foot?'

Shara didn't answer.

Jess's jaw dropped. 'Your parents spewed too, didn't they? Oh, Sharsy, they didn't...'

'Dad put Rocko on the float,' Shara said in a calm, controlled voice. 'He took him away.' She turned and began walking again. If she kept walking, she had to keep breathing. And if she could just keep breathing, in and out, she could keep the tears back.

Jess followed, leading Dodger behind her. 'For how long?'

Shara shrugged, bit her lip and kept walking.

'What? For good?' Jess swore in disbelief. 'They can't do that, he's *your* horse! You paid for him with your *own* money!'

'Oh, yes they can.' Shara looked ahead along the winding roadside track, putting one foot in front of the other, and changed the subject. 'Anyway, I'm more worried about Corey right now.'

'Did you go and see him? Is he okay?'

'No. Dad won't let me. But Tom's dad says he has concussion.' And that was when the tears burst. Shara stopped walking and let it all pour out. 'Corey is in real trouble and I've lost Rocko. You can't see Luke. All over one horse. It's all gone too far, Jess.'

Jess led her away from the road and found a large rock for them both to sit on. 'I should never have talked you into going to Brisbane. It was my stupid idea, but I didn't think ... I didn't realise how nasty the Connemans are.'

'They're saying we tried to steal the mare,' said Shara. 'They're saying she kicked Corey in the head. The whole thing is completely screwed up!'

'You're not wrong.' Jess sat quietly for a while. 'This all started out as a protest against wild horse races. It was about an event, not about one particular horse. Maybe we should just forget about Goldie, Shara.' She rubbed Shara's arm. 'The RSPCA will take good care of him. He's not your responsibility.'

'I know they will, but I can't let the Connemans get away with it. And where will Goldie end up if we don't help him? We've got everything we need to prove they own him, now.' Shara reached into her backpack and pulled out the small silk purse. 'I've still got the DNA sample, and the photo Corey took of the mare. She has a brand that proves she belongs to the Connemans. If we can show the colt is out of her, we can out those lying scumbags. It's really hard for me to get around without Rocko – could you take this to Tom's dad?'

'Why Tom's dad?' asked Jess, taking the purse.

'He said he would try to help Corey with the horse

theft charges. I reckon he might be able to use the sample as evidence that we were only after some hairs, not after the horse.'

Jess gave Shara a warm smile. 'I saw the way Corey fought for you. He's okay, I reckon.'

'Not just a rodeo schmuck?'

'He's a bit of a cowboy, if you ask me,' said her bestie. 'And you're right; it should be illegal to look that good in jeans. *Anyway*, I'll ride over to the Hoskins' place now and see if Tom's dad is home.'

'Ring me and tell me what he says.'

'Mum and Dad took my phone, as usual.' A look of misery crossed Jess's face. 'So that I can't ring Luke.'

'Oh, Jess. If we prove that we're the good guys, surely they won't hold you to that.'

Jess shrugged and Shara noticed how red raw her eyes were. She'd been bawling all night too. Shara gave her a hug. 'Hey, best bestie,' she said softly.

Jess gave her a feeble smile.

'We'll get these Connemans. Everything we need to redeem ourselves is in that purse.'

Jess buttoned it carefully into her top pocket, then put a foot in one stirrup and hoisted herself into the saddle. 'I'm working at the bakery this afternoon. Come down and I'll tell you what Mr Hoskins said.'

15

THE AROMA OF cinnamon buns seemed as wonderfully comforting as always when Shara walked into the bakery that afternoon. She took her place behind a thin woman with greying hair and waited for Jess to finish serving her.

Jess popped her head around the woman. 'Be with you in a sec, Shara.'

The woman turned and looked Shara up and down. Shara met her gaze. Her face had the deep-rutted wrinkles of a smoker. In her arms were two large paper sacks filled with day-old bread. She pushed past Shara, opened the doorhandle with her elbow and disappeared out the bakery door.

'Who was that?' Shara asked Jess.

Jess motioned for her to come closer. 'She's one of the Connemans, they're back in town,' she said in a hushed voice. 'She was asking all about you, even where you live!'

Shara went to the window and peeked between the net curtains. Some way down the street, the woman got into a small red sedan and closed the door. Shara recognised the car as the one that had nearly run her over that morning.

'Everyone in town is talking about Corey. They're all coming in here asking if he stole a horse.'

Shara snorted with outrage. 'The rumour mill is *unbelievable* in this town,' she said. 'What did Mr Hoskins say?'

'Not much. He said, "I'll see what I can do."' Jess held up her hands and shrugged.

Shara peeked back out the window. The car was still there, with two people sitting in the front. Her mind raced. 'What are they *doing* there?'

Jess joined her at the window. 'Stalking you, by the look of it.'

'Why?'

'Because they hate you?'

'Why? What did I do?'

'Errr, spray-painted all their brumbies, splashed them all over the front page of the local newspaper, forced them to surrender ten of their horses. Nearly put them out of business. Then there was the incident down in Brisbane...'

'Okay, *okay*! But it wasn't just *me*!'

'Yeah, but you're the one they busted.'

Shara cursed under her breath. This conversation was doing nothing to make her feel safer.

'Want me to ring the cops?'

'And tell them what?' said Shara. 'They're not doing anything wrong. They're just sitting in a car eating.'

A large white LandCruiser pulled up and parked behind the red car. John Duggin stepped out.

'Oh no, it's Corey's dad! He'll be so angry!' Shara briefly considered slipping out the back door.

'Is that the oven timer I can hear beeping?' said Jess, heading for the kitchen.

'Don't just leave me here,' hissed Shara.

John opened the door with such force that Shara thought the bell would jingle itself off its fixtures. He stalked to the counter and stared at the display of cakes with a tight face and his hands tucked into his dark-blue coveralls.

'Can I help you?' asked Jess, so meekly she sounded ridiculous.

John pulled a small plastic bag from his pocket and slapped it on the counter. Inside was the small lock of cream-coloured horse hair. So he had spoken to Mr Hoskins.

Shara stepped forward. 'Hi, John.'

John's eyes flashed to her. They were usually filled

with diagnostic contemplation and calm compassion. She had never seen him riled up before.

'Corey wasn't kicked by a horse,' he stated.

'No.'

'Why would someone punch him like that?' He turned the hair sample about in his hand, and Shara realised her answer would determine what he would decide to do with it. His eyes bored a hole through her. 'Did Corey throw the first punch?'

'Graham Conneman had me by the arm and Corey was trying to get him to let go.'

John's gaze didn't move from her as he digested her answer. 'Why did Graham Conneman have you by the arm?'

'He caught me mucking around with his horse, but we weren't trying to steal it, we were just trying to get that hair sample. We ran into Corey and he tried to tell me not to. He warned me that they weren't nice people.'

'You should have listened to him.'

'Yes.'

'You took this sample without the owner's consent?'

Shara nodded.

John tossed the bag into the rubbish bin that sat in the corner of the shop. 'Haven't you kids already been in enough trouble with these people without going searching

127

for more?' he said. Obviously he knew about the spray-painting.

'Hey!' Shara looked at the sample in the bin and thought of all she'd been through to collect it. 'We're not the bad guys! The Connemans are outside right now. Why don't you go and ask them what happened?'

'What?'

Shara pointed out the window. 'In the red car. You just walked straight past them!'

John stormed back out the door and marched across the road. Both Jess and Shara ran to the window and peeked out. The woman in the red car wound up her window and started the engine. The car jolted out of its park and John banged his fist on the bonnet as he jumped out of its way.

He stood in the street watching it disappear before marching back into the bakery, flinging the door open so hard that this time the bell really did fly off its fixtures. It landed on the floor with a limp jingle and rolled to a stop.

'Get in my car, Shara,' he ordered. 'I'll give you a lift home.'

Shara picked up her backpack, shot a farewell glance at Jess and followed him out the door.

John's four-wheel drive was huge, luxurious and smelled of pine deodoriser. She sank into the sheepskin-covered seat and pulled the lap sash around herself. John got in and the engine made a soft purr as he turned the key. He put the car into a U-turn and the ceiling-high racks of vet supplies rattled in the back. He cut the ABC news jingle on the radio.

'I'm really sorry that Corey got hurt,' said Shara.

'Don't be,' snapped John, flicking on the indicator and turning onto Coachwood Road. 'Might have done him some good, the smartalec.'

The silence was awkward as they drove along Coachwood Road.

'Have you seen Goldie?'

'Shara, that colt is the least of your concerns at the moment. You already have a good horse, you should concentrate on him.'

'Not anymore I don't.'

'What do you mean?'

'Dad took him away.'

John seemed taken aback and there was silence for a while. 'What, for good? Where did he take him? Not to the saleyards?'

John had been her vet when Shara had originally rescued Rocko. He'd seen what a soul-destroyed horse he was – he'd even been bitten by him. John was one person who had some connection with her story and had seen the amazing job she had done with Rocko. If he went to the sales, it would diminish a lot of John's efforts too.

'He took him to Blakely Downs, out past Longwood, to retire. It's a fifty-thousand-hectare property. Once they let him go, that'll be it. I won't see him again.'

John lifted his eyebrows. 'I thought parents only ever *threatened* to do that sort of thing.'

'Yeah, well, mine really did.' Shara felt a pain shoot through her chest. 'So, don't get on my case, because someone else is already heavily on it.'

John drove in silence for a while longer. He glanced in the rear-view mirror and Shara saw his expression change. He continued past the road to her place without turning off.

'Where are you going?'

'To the surgery. I have to check on the colt.'

There were four extra-large stables at the back of John's surgery. The walls were made of grey concrete and the windows of heavy-duty steel mesh. They were more like prison cells than stables. But maybe that was what Goldie needed. The colt hung his head out the door, tossed his nose up and down and nickered when he saw Shara. A smile broke across her face. He was so utterly charismatic. She held out a hand and he thrust his velvet muzzle into it, nibbling at her palm and then licking it. Goldie had filled out even more since she had last seen him and she realised he was going to be quite a tall horse: as tall, if not taller, than Rocko. His gloriously thick mane was still a messy tangle and Shara realised she had never had the chance to brush it in between disasters.

She took a matted piece of his forelock and untangled a large spiky burr from the middle of it. 'What's going to happen to you, Goldie?' she said quietly.

'He needs some exercise if you have a spare ten minutes,' said John from behind her. He held a syringe full of yellow stuff in one hand and a coiled rope in the other. 'I'll just give him his vitamin shot.'

John gave Goldie's neck a wipe with a swab and stuck the needle into his vein. He clipped the rope to the colt's halter and handed it to Shara. 'Just got to make a few calls and then I'll run you home.'

He disappeared into the office and Shara led Goldie out into the sunshine. There was a small paddock behind the surgery where she let him out onto the end of the rope to stretch his legs. Goldie burst into a canter. He pigrooted and squealed for five laps until Shara could pull him into a more controlled circle. He came back to an energetic trot and Shara grinned as she watched him fool around, tail high in the air and nose to the wind.

His colour was dazzling, a deep caramel with black dapples dancing down his hindquarters, shimmering in the sunlight. His silvery mane ruffled in the wind and caught the sun. His stride was playful and he reacted to Shara's movements with snorts and squeals and frolicking leaps. 'You've been locked up for too long,' she laughed, as he careered around on the end of the rope.

John appeared at the fence and waved her over. 'Got an emergency. I'll drop you home on the way.'

Shara reluctantly pulled Goldie to a stop and led him, prancing, back to the stable. He planted his feet outside the door, pulling against her.

'Come on, Houdini.' John gave him an encouraging slap on the rump and pushed him in through the doorway. He closed the door, pulled a padlock from his pocket and locked the top door securely.

John marched to the LandCruiser, and Shara had run after him.

John drove fast and Shara wondered what the emergency was. They hadn't gone far down the road when she saw the little red car come hurtling towards them.

John mumbled something under his breath and, once again, drove straight past Shara's street. 'Looks like you're coming with me again.'

'What are they *doing* in town?' said Shara.

'Looking for their colt.'

'Goldie?'

'That'd be the one.'

'I thought they denied owning him?'

'All of a sudden they want to pay his vet bills and claim him as theirs.'

'Why?'

'Well, that's the strange thing about people who neglect animals. They often still have a strong sense of ownership and entitlement over them. Now that they're looking like the victims, they think they might have a shot at getting him back.'

'Is that possible?'

He looked at her as he drove. 'Now they are saying that *you* stole him and *you* let him starve.'

'What?'

'Don't panic. We all know that's ridiculous. We're holding them off for as long as we can until we can work out what's going on. We certainly don't want to give him back if we don't have to.' He shot her a complicit grin. 'So much paperwork, y'know?'

'Do they know where he is?'

'Yes – the RSPCA was obliged to tell them.'

'They'll steal him back!' Shara twisted in her seat and watched the red car barrelling straight for John's place. Straight for Goldie. At least John had padlocked his stable, but that wouldn't stop the Connemans if they really wanted to take him. 'Shouldn't we go back?'

John nodded up ahead, to where another car zoomed

towards them, leaving big billows of dust in its wake. It was a police car. 'Don's already on the way. I just spoke to him on the phone. He won't let them take him.'

'How did he know?' She stared at John. 'Where are we going?'

'Like I said, there's been an emergency,' said John.

'Bigger than this one?'

'Yes.'

16

JOHN REACHED COACHWOOD ROAD, but instead of turning left into town, he turned right and made for the freeway.

They drove for more than half an hour and eventually turned into a narrow laneway. They reached a dilapidated building made from besser blocks, which looked as though it had once been a small dairy.

Shara unclipped her belt and followed John out of the car. The stench of stale horse urine and manure burned her nostrils. There was another foul smell too... something overpowering.

When she peered over the solid timber half-door, several wild-looking horses rushed to the other end of the building.

They were a heart-rending sight, thin and gaunt and utterly terrified. The smell, Shara realised, was a dead one over which they had all just trampled to get away from her. She dry-retched and put her hand over her mouth. 'Brumbies,' she gasped.

'Jesus Christ,' said John from behind her. 'Get straight back into the car and close all the windows. Just in case it's Hendra.'

Shara looked up at the big fig trees which hung over the old dairy block. They would have been planted there years ago to shade the dairy cattle, but these days they would be more likely to host huge colonies of bats, which feasted on the fruit and carried the deadly Hendra virus. Their droppings were all over the ground below and added to the foul smell.

Shara got back in the car and closed the door while John leaned against the back making phone calls. After a lengthy discussion he got back in the driver's seat. 'We'll have to wait for the police and the RSPCA to arrive before we try to move them,' he said. 'Sorry you had to see that, Shara.'

'Who do they belong to?'

'The Connemans, we think.'

'Are they brumbies?'

'I think so.'

Shara could hardly believe it. 'Now do you believe us?' she said, almost in tears again. She pointed out the window. 'Those people do that sort of thing and the whole town, including our parents, think *we're* the demons.

Why are you guys all so mad at us? Why aren't you mad at the *Connemans*?'

John held his hand up in a gesture that asked her to stop. She shut up, but breathed heavily with anger.

'You know, Shara,' John started. 'When I read about that spray-painting stunt in the paper, I thought it was great. I knew straight away who had done it and I thought it was gutsy.'

'And you didn't punish Elliot?'

'*What?*' said John. 'I didn't know *he* was involved!'

Whoops! Shara smiled weakly at John. 'He took the photos and emailed them to the newspaper.'

John exhaled loudly. 'That Grace Arnold. She's got him wrapped around her little finger.'

Shara suppressed a smirk. That was so true.

'Anyway, I knew it was your group of friends in general, what with Judy Arnold being an animal rescuer from way back and that Luke kid having such a strong liking for brumbies.'

'Actually, Luke wasn't involved in that bit.'

John huffed impatiently. 'The point I'm trying to make is that I agreed with you. With that bit, anyway. That stunt got a lot of people talking about brumbies and how they're treated. I grew up in the northern tablelands of New South Wales. Up there, nearly every station used the local wildies for stock work. The stockmen knew no other breed came close to them for toughness. I'd love to see more of them be re-homed instead of being turned into pet meat and used in rodeos.'

'People just think they're feral. No one cares about them.'

'A lot of people care very deeply about brumbies. But this sort of thing's not uncommon. They have such little monetary value and when they're fresh from the wild, they're hard to handle, so people just abandon them.'

'But all the buckjumpers and cattle are treated okay.'

'People like the Connemans treat most of their stock well because that's their business and they have to look after them. But the brumbies are bought cheap from the runners for the price of dog meat. They get rough-handled by the runners and come to the contractors out of their minds – and that's how the Connemans like them for rodeo, because it's more entertaining. When they're finished with them, it's cheaper and easier to just dump them; buy another lot later.'

John looked out the window at the bleak grey building. 'These horses are probably waiting for an abattoir to pick them up. The Connemans didn't bother leaving feed or water because they were going to die anyway.'

Shara was speechless. She stared out the car window and thought of the dismal creatures in that building, and then thought of Goldie galloping playfully around the paddock with his silvery mane flying in the breeze. 'That is so wrong.'

'Yes,' agreed John.

'So why the Hendra scare?'

'Because as soon as the authorities get here, the first thing they'll notice is that big fig tree full of bats. Hendra will be the first thing they have to rule out.'

Outside, an RSPCA van and two police cars rolled towards the dairy. John got out and started pulling on protective clothing from the back of his car.

Shara stayed put while John helped people in bright blue paper suits and face masks tape off a quarantine area with yellow ribbon.

Within half an hour the place was swarming with people, including some with cameras. Were they the media? How did *they* find out? The police seemed to be asking them to leave.

She rang her mum and told her where she was and what had happened. Louise insisted on coming to collect her immediately, making Shara promise faithfully not to contract any lethal viruses. As she hung up, John's phone rang on the seat beside her. She picked it up.

'John Duggin's phone.'

'Who's that?' said a vaguely familiar voice.

'It's Shara Wilson. John is tending to a horse right now. Can I take a message?'

There was a small pause before the person spoke again. 'Yeah, tell him Corey called.'

Shara reeled. She opened her mouth to speak, but nothing came out. Her mind whirled with questions. *Are you okay? Are you still in hospital?* While her mouth flapped soundlessly, there was an awkward silence as he waited for her to say something.

'Okay then? Bye.'

The phone disconnected before she could utter a word.

'No, wait!' She sat in the car, befuddled, wondering if she should call him back. Was he angry with her? Of course he was. He had taken a hit for her, protected her, probably saved her life, and she hadn't even managed to say hello to him. What must he think of her?

John opened the driver's door. 'I think we should get you home,' he said. 'This will take forever and we need to get all unnecessary people away from here.'

'Mum's already on her way.'

He nodded with approval.

'Corey rang. Wants you to ring him back.'

'Okay.' John nodded again, but his mind seemed somewhere else. His face carried a look of absolute disgust. 'I've come across some rank people, but these guys...' He seemed unable to find words for them.

Shara looked at the scene around the old dairy. The people in blue suits carried a large tarpaulin to cover the dead brumby's body. 'Poor thing.'

'What a waste of a beautiful horse,' said John.

'What will happen to the rest of the brumbies?'

'The RSPCA will contact some rescue groups and see if anyone can take them.'

Shara nodded, wishing she could take all of them, but they were so wild and freaked out, way beyond anything she could handle. 'God, I hope they don't get Goldie,' she thought out loud.

The lines deepened over John's brow and Shara saw a hardness in his eyes. 'No way am I going to let that happen.'

17

LOUISE WAS QUIET as she drove towards home, looking deeply troubled. Shara was glad that her mother had
seen the work of the Connemans with her own eyes this
time — she'd been horrified. Shara wondered what was
going through her mind. Finally Louise spoke.

'You know, part of me is really proud of you, Shara.'

'Really?' That was not what Shara had expected to
hear. So far her parents had made her feel like a complete
and utter piece of crap.

'To stand up for things that you believe in takes a lot
of courage, especially if others around you don't feel the
same way.'

Shara frowned. She didn't feel courageous. She just
felt stupid and confused.

'Your father and I went in a few protest marches when
we were at uni.'

'You're kidding.' Shara looked at her mum's hands on

the steering wheel. Her nails were manicured and she wore tasteful gold jewellery. Shara could hardly imagine her waving a placard around and chanting slogans.

'Student politics mostly, nothing too radical,' her mother continued. 'But it was easy to just join in a march when there were lots of other people alongside. What *you* did was really risky. I'd never have been brave enough to do something like that.'

So her mum was calling her a hero now. The day was getting more and more bewildering.

'What I *didn't* like was you putting your safety at risk. That was foolish.'

Shara nodded. 'So everyone keeps telling me.'

'You caused other people to get hurt.'

Okay, that bit she understood. She was back to being a complete and utter piece of crap.

Louise turned onto Coachwood Road and headed towards home.

Shara stared out the window and willed the road to go quickly. She just wanted to go home and hide in her room for the rest of the holidays. She wanted to go back to Canningdale College and not to have to think about all this.

'Don Bigwood wants me to take you down to the police station to make a statement.'

Shara groaned. 'Not another one!'

The Coachwood Crossing police station was a small timber building on stilts next to the railway station. It had a front desk, one small office behind a glass window and a tearoom off to the side.

Shara felt messy-minded and unclear as she tried to make sense of the afternoon's events. Outside, people were gathering and she could hear heated and excitable voices, Mrs Arnold's among them. Again, she was amazed at how quickly news spread through Coachwood Crossing, this time about the sick and dead brumbies.

Thank God Dad isn't home from out west yet. This would have really sent him over the edge.

The thought had barely formed in her head when the murmur of the crowd rose and the door of the police station burst open. Her father, red-eyed and bleary, walked straight to her. 'What happened?' he demanded.

Shara hadn't seen him since he had put Rocko and Goldie on the float and she could barely look him in the eyes. She turned away without replying.

'Did you do anything to further provoke those Connemans? Because if you did . . .'

'Hold on a minute, Barry,' said Sergeant Bigwood. 'The kid's done nothing wrong. We found some neglected animals on a remote property. We think they belong to the Conneman brothers.'

'Don, what are they doing back in town?' Barry's voice rose. 'I don't like them lurking around and stalking my daughter like this. What is going on?'

'Well, they wanted that colt back. But since then we've found this mob of wild brumbies, which complicates things.' Don went on to explain the afternoon's events. 'We're waiting for Hendra tests to see if the death of one of the horses was preventable or not.'

'Preventable or not?' Shara mumbled from her chair in the corner. 'You only have to look at the state the other horses were in to know it wasn't being cared for properly.' She muttered 'Hendra virus,' under her breath, adding a raspberry.

'Those brumbies were caught in the wild,' said Don Bigwood. 'The Connemans say they rescued them and were actually trying to get them back into good health for an upcoming rodeo.'

'*Oh, puh-leease!*' Shara snorted with disbelief. 'You don't honestly believe that, do you?'

'It doesn't matter what I believe,' said the sergeant sternly. 'What matters is the truth. Facts.'

'That brumby is dead. Doesn't get any more factual than that.'

'Yes, and we need to determine the cause of death

before we go jumping to conclusions. There are a whole lot of people who are not happy about what's happened, I know. But everyone needs to just calm down and go about things rationally and *legally*.'

Barry gave Shara a tight-lipped glare.

'*What?*' demanded Shara. 'How is a dairy full of sick and dead horses my fault? Those disgusting people should be run out of town. They should be hunted down and held accountable...'

'That's precisely what *shouldn't* be done, Shara,' said her father, his voice rising. 'That's exactly the type of thing I spoke to you about. That's a lynch-mob mentality, and completely against the law.'

'Well, some of the laws should be changed!'

'You can get change without breaking the law!'

'Well, *how*?' yelled Shara. 'The law hasn't been too good so far, has it? Everyone seems to know the Connemans are crooks, they treat their animals terribly, but they're still doing it, aren't they? Those horrible people are probably going to get Goldie back and the law is actually *protecting* them! Don't—'

'Hey, hey, *heyyy*!' yelled Sergeant Bigwood over the top of her, trying to calm them both down. 'I think you're both making a bit of sense,' he said. 'And if you'd put your heads together, you might find a solution to this whole problem. Blood samples have been taken and the cause of death will determine any cruelty charges.' He looked pointedly at Shara. '*If* there are any cruelty charges to be made.'

Shara shut her mouth and looked out the window.

'In the meantime,' Sergeant Bigwood continued in a quieter voice, 'it seems that stunt you pulled at the Coachwood Show has had some effect. A lot of people in this town support you and are angry about the Connemans' treatment of wild horses. Why don't you hold some sort of protest ride or something? It might put pressure on show societies to lift their game and stop using these guys as contractors.' He shrugged. 'The Kympania rodeo is on next weekend.'

Barry stood there, an intense look on his face. He breathed in. He breathed out. He looked to the ceiling. He looked to the door. He looked at Shara. 'Doesn't sound like a bad idea, actually.'

'Yeah, except I don't have a horse to ride,' said Shara.

Barry gave Shara a long, scrutinising look. For the briefest of seconds, she saw his face soften, before it hardened again. 'Borrow one.'

Sergeant Bigwood continued. 'You would need a written application to get a permit, but I can help you organise all that. Oh, and you'd need to contact the council as well.'

Shara sat, mouth tight.

'And you can organise it from somewhere else,' said

Sergeant Bigwood. 'I've got a station to run here.'

As they walked out the door, Shara looked at her father. His hair stuck up in a tufty crown around his bald patch and he looked exhausted, too tired to fight. So she plucked up the courage to ask about Rocko. 'Have they let him onto the station yet?'

'He's still in the house paddock,' said Barry. 'I want to see you put things right before we talk about him again.'

Shara knew by the look on his face and from past experience that he meant it. But his words offered her a faint glimmer of hope that she might see Rocko again. She forced herself to shut up, but she couldn't stop a fresh wave of tears running down her cheeks at the thought of him. She missed him dreadfully. She turned away and desperately tried to pull herself together. She would make things right. She had to.

That night Shara booted up her laptop and found about ten emails from Jess. Each one had a different version of **CONTACT ME!!!** in the subject bar. No sooner had she logged in than an instant message came up.

Sharsy, what happened? I haven't been allowed to

ring you. My email's going nuts with all the rumours –
is it true???
What have you heard?

Shara flopped onto her bed and curled up with her
computer. Her body was exhausted but her mind was
spinning like a flywheel. She gave Jess a run-down of
her day: told her about Goldie, the Connemans trying
to claim him back, about the dairy and the dead horse,
the brumbies, the trip to the police station. Jess fired
questions at her like a machine gun.

Did your dad spew? Do you reckon it's really Hendra?
OMG that's so scary!
**Jess I need your help. I want to run a protest ride about
cruelty to brumbies. The rodeo is on at Kympania this
weekend and there's a wild horse race on. I want the
protest ride to go past there.**

Jess quickly latched onto the idea. Rosie and Grace came
online and joined them in the chat, and before long they
were all tossing ideas around. Rosie suggested possible
meeting points:

We could start at the pony-club grounds and assemble
people there.

Jess thought of all the different clubs and horse organisations they could invite:

> We could look up different animal welfare people
> too – there are lots of brumby groups!

And then Grace had an epiphany.

> Hey, Kympania is near the mountains. We could do a
> mountain ride – a brumby ride – how excellent would that
> be!!! We could run a sausage sizzle afterwards!

A brumby ride – perfect. Grace was a genius. They would ride past the Kympania rodeo, up through the mountains for a picnic lunch and then finish by riding back through the main street of Kympania. They decided to meet the following evening at the pony club with as many people as they could muster to discuss the finer details.

18

BARRY JANGLED HIS KEYS and opened the door of the little timber clubhouse, flicking on the lights as he stepped into the doorway. Shara stepped in behind him. A waft of cool air and old cooking smells mixed with seasoned timber greeted them.

Barry walked straight to the hot water urn and lifted the lid. 'How do I get this thing to work?'

'Let the expert have a look,' Shara said. She flicked the switch at the power point and turned the knob at the front of the urn. 'There you go: it'll take about fifteen minutes.'

Vehicles began to fill the pony club grounds one by one. It had taken only a few text messages and tweets for the word to spread like lightning. Cars, utes, old trucks and four-wheel drives lined up in rows. Doors slammed and voices called hello.

Barry did blokey farm talk with John Duggin and Lawson Blake. They were soon joined by Ian Hoskins.

Tom and Rosie arrived in Tom's sleek black ute, and Grace and Elliot turned up squeezed onto Elliot's tiny motorbike with their knees around their ears. Anita from the animal shelter came with a group of colleagues and before long they were joined by Lurlene Spencer, who wore violent red lipstick like war paint. Shara wasn't surprised to see her chatting with Judy Arnold as if they were old friends.

Pony club members turned up by the dozens, keen to help out any horses in trouble. Other locals leaned against fence posts and tucked their hands in their pockets as they talked. They had all seen or at least heard about the protest against the wild horse race at this year's show, and were beginning to admit they had loved it. They knew about the dead brumby at the dairy, and the colt at the vet surgery, although Anna Paget grumbled that Goldie should stay there permanently.

'Okay, let's get this meeting going,' Barry called out over the crowd. 'Can everyone come and sit down?' The crowd shuffled around, finding seats and standing room. Barry sat at the front bench and was flanked by Shara, Jess, Rosie, Grace and Sergeant Bigwood.

As the noise level settled to a low mumble, the sergeant stood and addressed the crowd.

'As you may have heard, some very sick horses were found by the RSPCA yesterday. Now, rather than forming a lynch mob, Barry and these girls have come up with a plan to hold a protest ride this weekend. The Conneman brothers will be supplying brumbies for the wild horse race at Kympania and that will be our starting point. This is a legal way to go about raising concerns for brumby safety, especially in wild horse races.'

Barry stood up next to Sergeant Bigwood. 'We appreciate everyone being here, but if anyone feels they can't work with us without causing trouble, they may as well leave now. This is going to be a peaceful ride.'

There were murmurs. Several people turned and stared at Judy Arnold, who stood tight-lipped and frowning, her hands clenched in her pockets. 'What?' she growled.

Barry continued. 'Right, now let's organise this ride.' He turned to Shara. 'Are you taking notes?'

'Yep,' said Shara, pen in hand.

Sergeant Bigwood gave the crowd a run-down of what they needed to do about the applications and permits in order to ride through town. Then Barry began to delegate jobs. Shara wrote furiously, making lists of people to contact and recruit. They would ring every pony club secretary in the district and ask them to contact their members. The RSPCA, the local campdrafting club and adult riding club members would all be notified. There would be an advertisement in Friday's paper as well.

Elliot offered to set up a Facebook page, and Rosie was

placed in charge of arranging parking at the Kympania Pony Club and fresh water for the horses. Jess was made publicity officer, responsible for contacting the media. Grace would organise the sausage sizzle and Tom volunteered to help draw up a petition to present to the mayor.

A clipboard was passed around for people to record their names and phone numbers so they could be contacted to help. The details were endless, but Shara remained sharp and alert, writing furiously, not missing anything. Her mind raced and her excitement grew.

'I can't believe how much support we're getting,' she said to her father on the way home.

'Yeah, you can tell not much ever happens in this town. It's like a re-run of the fete,' said Barry.

'You don't think it's because they believe in us?'

'That too – a bit of both, I reckon. Most decent people don't like to see animals suffer, but they don't often get up and do much about it.' Barry went quiet for a moment and then he glanced at his daughter. 'That prank of yours was wrong, but not as wrong as what the Connemans did to Corey, or to those brumbies.'

Shara was silent for a while, soaking up the relief she felt that her dad was coming around.

'Thanks for helping me with the brumby ride.'

'Well, I've always said parenting is not about punishing but about teaching your kid to do the right thing. You've still got a big job ahead of you to put things right.'

She nodded and thought of Corey. She had a big job ahead to put things right with him, too.

19

THE DOOR TO THE Duggins' sprawling Queenslander home was wide open and Shara could hear a telly. She stood outside on the verandah and knocked. 'Hello?'

Corey's voice echoed down the hallway from an inner room. 'Yeah?'

She kicked off her boots and crept along the floorboards in her socks, following the voice. 'Corey?'

'In here.'

Shara peered through an open bedroom door at Corey, who sat cross-legged in jeans on a bed, a remote in his hand, staring at a small television. She quickly withdrew when she registered that he had no shirt on.

'It's Shara,' she said, hovering at the doorway. No one else seemed to be home.

The telly volume lowered. 'Come in.'

His arms and head were halfway through an old T-shirt when she entered. When they popped out, she saw that the side of his face was heavily bruised. 'What are you doing here?'

'What are *you* doing here?' she smiled.

'Got the crap smacked out of me,' he said, stating the obvious. 'Told you those Connemans were bad news.' He didn't seem happy. At all.

Shara stood there, with her bag hooked over her shoulder, wondering if she should sit down. He didn't invite her to. 'I'm so sorry, Corey,' she said, switching tone.

He didn't answer but stared back at the television. She took the swivel chair by a desk strewn with old videos and DVDs, and put her bag on the floor.

It was a while before Corey spoke again. 'I can't even remember what happened.'

'Can you remember being at the roping finals?'

He shifted his eyes to hers. 'Some of it.'

'Do you remember plucking the mare?'

He frowned with concentration, then snorted suddenly. 'You fell off the side of the truck.'

'Yep.'

'You fall off everything.'

'Except my horse.' She shrugged.

Then his frown returned. 'I remember that lanky vermin Conneman getting hold of you. He was hurting you.'

'He would have hurt me more if you hadn't fought him off.'

'Yeah, well, I hope I got him good,' Corey said, looking at the bandage over his broken knuckles and then putting it up to his swollen cheek. 'He got *me* a ripper!'

'You got him pretty good,' she assured him. 'Enough to make him let go of me. Then the other brother king-hit you. It was two against one.'

His frown deepened and he stared hard at the floor. 'Nope, don't remember that part.'

'You were a bit of a hero,' she said quietly.

He lifted his eyes. 'Was I?' He sounded unsure of himself.

She nodded. 'Thanks for saving me.'

His gaze ran over her and she could see he was still wrestling with his memory.

'Graham had me by the arm. He was calling me names and wouldn't let go,' she said, trying to help him picture the scene. 'You flew at him, gave him one in the jaw.'

Corey looked at his bandaged hand. 'I can't believe I did that.'

'You didn't hesitate.'

Corey began to look quite pleased with himself. 'Yeah?'

'Took two of them to fight you off.'

He gave her a heart-melting smile and the crescent-shaped bruise around his eye merged with the one on his cheek. 'You're just trying to make me feel good!'

'It's true.' She saw the same amused twinkle in his eyes

that she had seen in them that day at the Coachwood Crossing Show, when she had just gone tail-up off the fence.

'You're sweet,' he said, shifting around to face her more directly, 'and funny . . . in a klutzy kind of way.'

She felt suddenly awkward. 'I'm a troublemaker.'

'There's something I do remember,' he said, as though weighing up whether to tell her or not.

'What?'

He hesitated.

'*What?*' she repeated.

His voice softened. 'I can remember how much I wanted to kiss you when those security guards walked past.'

She looked away, blushing hotly. 'You laughed at me.'

'No, I didn't.'

There was an uncomfortable moment as she tried not to meet his gaze, instead taking in his tanned neck and the way his T-shirt fell over the broad contours of his shoulders.

'I still want to kiss you,' he said.

She allowed her eyes to meet his, and she felt that mix of thrill and fear again – fear that if she let herself fall into their warm hazel depths she'd fall so far and so hard that she might never be able to climb out.

'You want to kiss all the girls.'

'No, I don't.' He gave a hopeless shrug. 'They want to kiss *me*.'

She scoffed, trying to diffuse the awkwardness she felt. Suddenly the room seemed to suffocate her. She needed to get out of there. 'My point exactly,' she said.

He put out a hand to stop her. 'Just hang out with me, then. I'm so bored.'

'Only if we go outside. Your room smells like old socks.'

There was an old couch on the verandah, covered in dog hair, bridles and dirty jumpers. Scattered about were boots, more dog hair and more stinky socks.

'Place is a bit of a bachelor pad,' said Corey apologetically. 'Between me, Dad and Elliot, it doesn't get a lot of sweeping.' He reached into a large fridge with stickers all over it and pulled out two cans of cola. 'Want one?'

He brushed all the clutter off the couch, plonked down into it and crossed his legs again.

Shara took the can, sat next to him and put her feet up on an old milk crate. 'Where's your mum?'

'Lives in Brissie.'

Shara cracked her can. 'Well, here's to her!'

'Cheers,' agreed Corey, taking a long, thirsty guzzle.

Shara looked back along the tree-lined driveway. On either side were small post-and-rail paddocks with bandaged horses and baby calves. Nearer the house, an offshoot led to the surgery. From that direction came the sound of feet crunching over gravel.

As Shara sat shoulder-to-shoulder with Corey, a girl

appeared, her legs as thin as pencils in skin-tight black jeans. She wore a collared shirt tucked in under a rodeo buckle and a peaked cap with a black ponytail poking out the back; she looked vaguely familiar.

The girl's eyes narrowed when she saw Shara and darted back to Corey.

Shara smiled, trying to look friendly. *Awkward!*

Her smile wasn't returned.

Corey spoke first. 'Hi, Mandy.' He didn't move from the couch.

Mandy stood there without speaking, her face pinched.

Shara stood up and offered her hand, since Corey was making no attempt to introduce her. 'I'm Shara.'

'*Shara?*' Mandy glared at her, and then at Corey. 'What's going on, babe?'

Babe? Shara retracted her hand.

Mandy's glare was firmly locked on Corey.

'I should probably get going,' said Shara, looking around for her bag. Corey was fine, and obviously had plenty of company. She'd apologised and set things straight, so there was no further reason to hang about. She realised she had left her bag ... *argh* ... in Corey's room. *Not good!*

Corey saw her searching. 'You left your bag in my bedroom,' he said, without getting up.

Shara felt herself shrivel with embarrassment. Corey

161

made it sound like they'd been *doing* something in there. He was using her as a weapon against this Mandy girl! She had no idea what was going on between them, but she had no intention of getting involved.

'Maybe you could go and get it for me then,' she said icily.

Her tone must have reached Corey, because he pulled himself off the couch, went inside and resurfaced a moment later with her bag. 'Sorry,' he said to her quietly.

Shara hopped off the balcony and marched back along the driveway, slinging her bag over her shoulder. When she got to the first easement, she ran down through the long grass and sprinted across the river flats to the creek.

There, she sat on a smooth rock platform and watched the water slither and gurgle over the pebbles, trying to digest what had just happened.

Schmuck!

'How's Corey?' asked Louise, when Shara walked onto the verandah at home later that morning.

'Not all that great,' said Shara.

She threw herself into the hammock and curled its edges up around her, hiding her face. She thought of

Mandy's cold glare. *'Shara?'* Mandy had known who she was. How?

And Corey. Did he mean all those nice things he said, or was he just a charmer to everyone?

Shara flashed back to before Mandy had shown up; his warm, easy smile. *'I can remember how much I wanted to kiss you.'*

She hadn't been brave enough, or stupid enough, she now realised, to tell him she had felt the same. She thought of his breath on her neck again, when he'd pushed her against the side of the truck at the Brisbane showgrounds and whispered to her. She closed her eyes and relived the clean smell of him.

Then she forced her eyes open. She had to stop thinking this way about him. Corey was a player. God, how much more proof did she need? Mandy was at his place now, probably with her paws all over him. *'What's going on, babe?'*

Shara shook her head and tried to focus on the brumby ride. She didn't need distractions. But there was the vision of Corey again, leaning into her, whispering softly in her ear, apologising for getting too close, when all she'd wanted to do was reach up and kiss him.

Arghhhh! She had to stop this. *Focus, woman!*

His complete lack of hesitation when it came to protecting her...

'*Shara?*'

'Huh?' Shara snapped back to earth. 'Sorry, what?'

'I asked if you'd like to visit the colt this afternoon,' said Louise. 'John rang and said he needs people to exercise him because he's locked up.'

Shara peered over the edge of the hammock. 'Oh, can we?'

That would be great – as long as she didn't have to go anywhere near the Duggins' house. Yay! Things were turning around!

Horses – so much easier to understand than boys!

20

THEY FOUND GOLDIE under lock and key when they got to the surgery. Two extra padlocks had been added to his stable and there was a strip of checked blue tape across the wire mesh of the upper door.

Goldie recognised Shara instantly and began tossing his head and whinnying. She tried her best to pat his nose through the mesh and he nipped playfully at her fingers, banging at the stable door with his hoof.

Shara went to John's office and found Elliot under the desk fiddling with the leads of a computer. She noticed a framed studio photo of the two boys: Elliot, aged about seven, and Corey about ten. They actually looked like brothers: Elliot without his glasses and with the same dark hair as Corey. How different they were now.

Elliot crawled out from under the desk and blinked up at her through his specs. 'Hi, Shara.'

'Hi,' she smiled. Elliot was always so earnest and

genuine. Unlike his big brother. 'I need the keys to Goldie's stable. Your dad said I could exercise him.'

'Oh, sure.' Elliot got up and went to a nailboard full of keys. He grabbed a set and handed them to her. 'There's a lunge rope hanging outside the stable. I would do it, but the office modem just blew up. I told Dad I'd fix it.'

'That's okay.' Shara had seen Elliot trying to lunge horses before.

'I'm more of a cat person,' he said apologetically.

She laughed. 'I'll give him a good work-out.'

'Don't let him off the rope, whatever you do.'

'Yep.' Shara ran off towards the stables.

Goldie exploded out of his stall.

'Whoa,' gasped Shara, holding onto his halter. He was a *lot* stronger and heavier. She led him, prancing and snorting and tossing his tangled silver mane, out to the small exercise paddock.

'I'm going to groom you too,' she said, as she let him out onto the full length of the rope.

Goldie burst away from her and galloped as hard and fast as his legs would carry him for about ten laps. He bucked and farted and then broke back into a trot, tail high and waving like a flag, nose swinging from side to side. Shara let him play and get it all out of his system, and Goldie ran and ran as if he hadn't been out for weeks. Each time Shara thought he was beginning to slow down a bit, he took off with a whole new level of energetic bucking.

Finally, he propped into an abrupt halt, puffing heavily, all four feet planted beneath him. He dropped his head and faced her with a pleased look. Shara laughed. 'You're an idiot.'

Goldie walked to her and tossed his nose up and down, giving Shara an idea. She reached into her pocket, pulled out a few of the pellets she had taken from the feedroom, clicked her tongue and treated him. Every time Goldie tossed his head, she clicked and treated him. Then she added a cue.

'Are you an idiot?' She held the pellet under his nose, then raised it up and down to make him nod before she gave it to him.

Within minutes, Goldie understood and nodded on cue. 'Are you a clever horse?' Shara asked, using the same tone. He nodded again. She gave him a pat on the neck and led him back towards the stable. 'Shall I make you beautiful?' Goldie nodded and then boofed her in the back.

'Sorry, I've run out of pellets,' she laughed.

She found a dribble of shampoo in an old bottle at the horse wash and squeezed the last of it over Goldie, rubbing it into a lather and slopping it through his filthy mane. Brown dirty water ran out of him as she rinsed him off. She pushed her fingers into the bone of his tail and got out all the scungy bits. Finally she sponged his head clean and wiped around his muzzle and eyes.

When she had finished, both of them were soaking wet, so she led him out into the sunshine and let him shake like a huge dog. His water-soaked mane flap-flap-flapped against his neck, flinging water everywhere. She scraped him off and rubbed him all over with a towel and he lifted his lip and waggled it with appreciation. Then she set to on his mane, combing out all the burrs and matted bits, and brushing it until the silvery streaks dazzled. She did the same with his tail and snipped it into a neat bang.

As the last damp patches on his pelt faded, she trotted him out on the lunge rope again and marvelled at his glossy smooth coat. He had the muscle and athleticism of a quarter horse, the sharp mind of a trick horse and the hardiness and wily charms of the Australian brumby – and the mix of his parents had given him that beautiful and rare silver taffy colour. Galloping about, freshly washed and groomed in the sunlight, Goldie was absolutely and totally the most spectacular horse Shara had ever laid eyes on.

'We have to get you out of here, Goldie,' Shara said, when the little colt trotted back to her and rested his head in her arms. 'You're too special to be in a stupid rodeo.'

She changed to her training tone. 'Is that a good idea?' But Goldie didn't nod. He pushed into her, twisted his head a little and closed his eyes.

She rubbed his cheeks and kissed him in the little hollow above his eyes. 'You won't be stuck in here much longer,' she promised.

Shara spent the next day at home, organising the brumby ride with her friends. Grace and Elliot came over and helped her turn the sunroom into an office. Jess's parents, although reluctant, let her come and help too.

'You know, all these plugs and cables are totally un-necessary these days,' said Elliot, crawling out from under the desk. 'Cloud computing is way better.'

'Don't care, as long as I can google,' said Shara. 'Let's look up the Connemans.'

She and Jess sat side-by-side in front of the computer and began by searching 'Conneman brothers'.

'Hey, check this out,' said Jess. 'Mark Conneman has a two-year banning order for failing to provide veterinary care for sick and injured animals.'

'Why doesn't that surprise me?' said Shara. 'What about the other one – Graham?'

She took the mouse and keyboard from Jess and

googled 'Graham Conneman': lots of rodeo photos, bucking broncos, team roping photos.

'Stop, stop!' said Jess suddenly. 'That one said something about a Mandy Conneman. Go back!'

Shara scrolled back up. *Surely not*.

And then she saw it. *'Mandy Conneman takes out the junior roping at Dunega.'* That was her all right, in her skin-tight jeans on a bay horse.

'So that Mandy girl was Graham Conneman's daughter?' said Jess.

'Oh my God.' Shara thought of Corey riding alongside her at the Coachwood Crossing Show, the two of them bumping their horses against each other. 'That lying, sleazy, rodeo *schmuck*!'

'I'll say!'

Shara shoved her chair away from the desk and took herself to the bathroom. Corey was going out with *Graham Conneman's daughter*? No wonder Mandy had given her a daggers look when she'd introduced herself!

She went out to the lounge room, where Grace and Elliot were setting up the Facebook pages. 'Did you know Corey goes out with Mandy Conneman? Graham Conneman's daughter.'

Elliot glanced up from his laptop. 'Dad and I don't like her much.' He shrugged. 'She's not very nice.'

'How come you never told me?'

Elliot looked at her through his thick-rimmed glasses. 'She's not his girlfriend or anything. She just kind of hangs around him. Heaps of girls do.'

'Corey's a sleaze,' said Grace. 'Oh, sorry, Elliot.'

But Elliot seemed uninterested, and turned back to the photos he had just uploaded.

Shara channelled her fury by getting back to work on the brumby ride. She and Jess found a photo of a horse being pulled to the ground and composed a flyer with the heading:

WILD HORSE RACE – A TOTAL DISGRACE!

They included the date, place and time of the brumby ride, and sent it to every newspaper, television and radio station in the district.

'Who else can we send it to?' Shara said, still dissatisfied. 'We need people to come along.'

'How about animal welfare groups?' said Jess. 'There are heaps of those.'

Grace peered over their shoulders. 'Mum reckons they have info packs for people holding rallies.'

The girls soon discovered that there were many organisations and groups on the internet offering information and support for people holding events. They collected the contacts for as many organisations as they could find, emailed them the brumby ride flyer and invited their members to come along. They asked for emails, faxes and letters of support that they could forward to the local council, demanding that all wild horse races be banned from rodeos.

'Hey, look, we can do an online petition!' said Shara. 'We could get signatures from people all over the country!'

'So even if they can't come to the ride, they can lend us their voice!' said Jess.

'We still need lots of people to come on the brumby ride,' said Shara, 'or it won't make a good news story.'

'Let's ask people to come on foot!' suggested Grace.

'Reckon they'd come?'

'We could ask,' Grace shrugged.

'This is going to be huge!' said Jess, with a worried half-smile.

'I hope so,' grinned Shara.

Shara and Jess spent the rest of the week pinning up posters around town. Elliot made a website to Grace's design specifications. Tom and Rosie walked the streets collecting more signatures for the petition to the mayor.

It seemed the whole town was abuzz with preparations. Annie Blake rang to say she had been baking all day with the ladies from the CWA and would be bringing 'refreshments' to the sausage sizzle. Chan, Jess's boss at the bakery, offered to donate the bread.

Mrs Arnold was keen to be part of any horse-rescue operation. She offered to help by being their official taxi driver, ferrying them in and out of town to pick up sausages and cans of soft drink for the sausage sizzle.

The phone rang continually. 'Brumby Ride Hotline!' Shara sang, snatching it from its cradle.

'I got two more people coming!' said Jess on the other end.

'Did you find out how many are coming from the trail ride club?'

'About eight.'

By the end of the week Shara's inbox was full of responses from animal welfare groups. As she looked down the long list of emails, she punched the air victoriously. *Yes!* She printed them out and put them in a large envelope addressed to the mayor.

'Heaps of people are coming,' said Shara over the phone to Jess again, looking at her final list. 'A hundred people is just a rough estimate, there'll also be people who'll just turn up on the day.' She rubbed her hands together in anticipation. 'Connemans, here we come!'

21

THE MORNING BEFORE the ride, Shara was woken by her phone ringing. She groped around for it on her bedside table without taking her head off the pillow.

'Shara.'

'Corey?' What did *he* want?

'Hi.' He sounded uncharacteristically hesitant.

'How are you?' she asked cautiously.

'Getting better. Still not allowed to ride or drive a car.'

'Sounds boring.'

'It is,' he said flatly. 'Elliot keeps trying to give me his electronic games to play with.'

'When can you ride?'

'One more day. It's just a precautionary thing. I feel fine.'

The conversation hit a lull and Shara tried to think of more small talk. What did this have to do with her? Why was Corey ringing her with his problems? Why didn't he ring *Mandy*?

'Why are you ringing me?' she finally asked.

There was a pause. 'I felt bad . . . about Mandy being here, when you came over.'

'Why? It's a free world.'

'Mandy is Graham Conneman's daughter.'

'I know.'

'She hangs around me all the time. She seems to think we've got something going. I don't know why, I keep telling her . . .'

'Oh, well, thanks for explaining that.'

'Shara, I don't even like her.'

'Whatever. Nothing to do with me.'

Shara wished he'd just shut up. Her head started spinning again. Why did he do this to her all the time? Did he like making an idiot out of her? Did he have some sick need to reel girls in and have them hang off him? Well, she wasn't into it. She didn't care if he looked like some sort of demigod; she had no desire to be part of his little harem.

'The Connemans own Sampson,' said Corey. 'I can't just be rude to her.'

'I thought Sampson was your good horse.'

'He *is* my good horse, but I don't own him. He's an open campdraft winner, trained for roping and barrel racing – an insanely good horse. It's been a real honour to ride him. I'd never have placed in the Nationals without him.'

'So you've sold your soul to ride a good horse?'

There was a tense pause on the end of the line. 'Not anymore. Graham's taking him back. They're picking him up this afternoon.'

Shara felt a rush of guilt. That was *her* fault. 'I'm sorry, Corey. I never meant for you to get tangled up in this. I never asked you to . . .'

'I know you didn't, but I wanted to.'

There was a silence. 'Why?'

'I like you,' he said simply. 'You're funny. And sweet.'

'And klutzy.'

She heard him exhale. 'Is it so hard for you to believe that I might like you?'

'No, not at all, you like heaps of girls.' Shara instantly regretted her bitchy tone. She sucked in a deep breath and switched back to aloof ice queen.

'That's a bit harsh, Shara.'

'What do you want me to say?'

Corey was quiet for a while. 'Not that.'

It was all so confusing. Shara needed Jess here, to advise her on all this boy stuff. She snuggled into her doona and had the sudden urge to reach through the phone and touch him. She wondered if he was shirtless again, sitting cross-legged and barefoot in old jeans. And then the thought of Mandy on his verandah, glaring at her, ruined the image.

'I can't bear the thought of the Connemans getting Goldie back,' she finally said.

'I can't bear the thought of them getting Sampson back.'

'I suppose you heard about the brumby ride.'

'I did,' said Corey. 'Good for you. If I can find a horse to ride, I'll join you.' He seemed relieved at the change of subject. 'Are you taking the colt along, as a token brumby?'

So he didn't know. The thought of Goldie sliced through her. 'He won't be there. I don't have him anymore.'

'Really? I thought you were going to buy him or adopt him or something.'

'Yeah well, that was before Dad got called down to Brisbane in the middle of the night by the police.'

She heard Corey inhale. 'Your old man sent him away?'

'Both of them. Rocko's out at Blakely Downs and Goldie is with your dad at the surgery until they can sort out who owns him. Didn't John tell you?'

'Oh, Shara,' he said softly. 'I didn't know. I haven't been over to the surgery. Dad's been so gnarly, he's barely spoken to me. That's ruthless.'

'Guess I deserved it.'

'Reckon?' He sounded stunned.

Shara decided not to dwell on it and cheered herself up by telling him about all the people who were coming to the brumby ride. She talked and he listened.

'Mr Hoskins wants me to counter-sue Graham Conneman. He said he'd represent me for free,' Corey told her when she finished.

'You should go for it. He deserves it.'

'But I can't remember what happened.'

'I can,' said Shara. 'I can remember all of it.'

Later that morning, the house phone rang. Shara dived on it. 'Brumby Ride Hotline—'

'Shara.'

'John?'

'Do you want the good news or the bad news?'

'Good,' she said. 'I don't think I could handle any more bad news.'

'The dead brumby tested negative for Hendra, so we can pursue cruelty and neglect charges against the Connemans.'

'That's great,' exclaimed Shara. 'I knew it!' She looked out the window to where her dad sat on the balcony, having a cuppa. She couldn't wait to tell him and vindicate herself.

'But it also means the brumbies from the dairy are cleared from quarantine and technically they can be used at the rodeo this weekend for the wild horse race – unless we can get charges on the Connemans before that. But I doubt we can.'

Shara's heart sank. Those poor wretched creatures would be completely traumatised. By the time the wild horse race was over they would be beyond any hope of a relationship with humans. They would be dog mince. 'Is there any more news on Goldie?'

'Yes – the Connemans have surrendered ownership.'

'Yay!' Shara jumped around, tangling herself in the phone cord and victory-punching the air. 'Yes! Yes! Yes!'

'The paperwork came through this morning, so I got the gelding done straight away.'

Shara immediately had visions of the little taffy horse grazing alongside her dad's cattle in the front paddock. 'What will happen to him?' she asked excitedly, letting hope rise inside her. 'Will they re-home him?'

She felt a surge of determination; to make things right; to run this brumby ride with all she had. She would show her dad that she could do the right thing, that she deserved to have that beautiful silver taffy colt – no, gelding!

'He's already gone to a new home.'

'What?' Shara felt her chest collapse like a pricked

balloon. 'New home?' She stood bewildered, staring at the phone. 'What do you mean? Where?' She glanced out the window at her dad, absorbed in his newspaper.

'It's a really nice place in New South Wales. It was such a good deal for him with such a kind family that we thought we should seize it. It's what's best for Goldie.'

Shara was struck dumb.

'You do want what's best for him, don't you?' said John.

'Yes,' said Shara, in a choked voice. 'Of course I do.'

She hung up the phone and opened the screen door to the balcony. 'You knew, didn't you? You let John give Goldie away.'

Barry finished turning a page of his paper, lifted his glasses from his nose and looked at her. He spoke in an irritatingly calm voice. 'I told you, I won't discuss the horses until you've shown that you can do the right thing.'

Shara turned on her heel, let the screen door crash back into its frame and ran to her bedroom. She slammed her door with a bang that reverberated through the entire house, and threw herself on the bed.

22

HER COMPUTER PINGED.

> Sharsy, what time do the CWA ladies have to deliver
> their cakes tomorrow?

'Oh, Jess.' Shara wiped her eyes. She couldn't care less
about the stupid cakes. She typed back.

> **John just rang, he's already re-homed Goldie.**
> What the...

Shara sniffed and continued hammering on the keyboard.
Her hands shook as she typed.

> **He's gone to a new home in NSW.**
> OMG, that was quick.
> **Dad already knew. He had it lined up.**

I can't believe it.

I didn't even get a chance to prove myself!

There was a knock on her door and Shara went stiff.

Another knock.

'What?' she demanded.

'Shara, I want to talk to you,' said her father's voice.

'Go away,' she sobbed back.

The door slowly opened and Barry stood in the doorway with one hand on the knob. 'I said, I want to talk to you.'

Shara closed her laptop to hide her chat with Jess and stood up to face him, her arms folded tightly across her chest. 'This isn't fair and you know it,' she said tearfully. 'You know that the Connemans are cruel and dodgy. You know that they're the bad guys; that they let their horses suffer. Why are you still being so cruel to me? You've taken everything that I love!'

'Don't get melodramatic,' said Barry quietly. 'You can still hold that brumby ride and then we can talk about the horses.'

'Hold the brumby ride?' said Shara. 'What's the point now? What's the point of anything? I have no horses left. Rocko is gone forever and so is Goldie. What's left to talk about?'

Barry folded his arms, no give in his expression. 'So

that's what this ride is all about?' he said. 'It's all about you. Not about helping brumbies or about preventing cruelty. It's all about you and your own horses.'

'You don't get it, Dad!' she yelled. 'I don't even have a horse to ride!'

'Can't you borrow one?'

'What for? I told you, there's no point!'

'There *is* a point,' said Barry. 'You did something wrong. What the Connemans do or don't do doesn't change that. You still need to put it right. Just because they're crooks, it doesn't give you the right to be a crook as well.'

Shara looked her father in the eye and let her tears stream down her face. She wanted him to see what this was doing to her. 'Can't I at least have Rocko back? He's too young to retire. I need him. If I can have him back, I can still ride. Without him, I just can't... I can't even live.'

At last she saw Barry's face soften. 'Shara.' He stepped forward and tried to rub her arm. She pushed his hand away and stood with her arms wrapped tightly, protectively around herself.

Barry sighed long and deep.

'This is too harsh, Dad.'

'Even if I did say you could take Rocko in the brumby ride, I couldn't go and get him. There's no time. The four-wheel drive is back at the mechanic's again and I can't tow a horse float with your mother's car.'

Shara looked to the ceiling. It was just hopeless.

'I'll leave it up to you as to whether you continue with the brumby ride. But if you do decide to cancel, you'll have to let all the riders know pretty quickly. It's on tomorrow.' He left the room, closing the door behind him.

Shara threw herself back on the bed and lay staring at the ceiling. Her phone rang. She ignored it. After it had rung out, a text message came through.

I can ride and drive again! Finally!

As if she cared. She thumbed Corey a message.

Lucky you.

She flung the phone at the wall, picked up her jacket and stormed out the front door of the house.

Her feet tumbled one after the other down the steep grassy paddock, startling and breaking up the mob of weaners. The setaria seeds whipped at her bare arms, outstretched to balance herself as she hurtled down to the creek, hoping that, somehow, she could outrun the hurt and confusion that was chasing her. Hex gambolled along behind, his tail rotating like a propeller.

Shara followed the cattle trail that ran along the cool water's edge, in and out of mossy-trunked trees and clumps of strappy lomandra grass, until she was halted by a barbed-wire fence. She slipped under it and ran across the lightly timbered hillside of the neighbouring property.

At Mr Hickling's orchard she slowed to a walk, puffing heavily, still trying to blow away the ache in her chest. She continued past the rows of lychee trees, skirting a discarded fruit-collecting tub and a stack of white buckets that had fallen over. Lorikeets flew in and out of the trees, screeching and squawking.

Beyond, the land sloped down into Slaughtering Creek and Shara stepped along a slippery log that had made a bridge across the smooth-running water. On the other side a trail ran along the creek and then up a hillside where the trees became gradually smaller and sparser.

At the top of Mossy Mountain, she sat heavily on her favourite rock, with her arms wrapped tightly around her knees and her eyes squeezed closed, feeling streaks of cold where the breeze dried her tear-soaked cheeks. She swallowed, opened her eyes and let the view snatch her breath away as it always did. The Coachwood River meandered through the valley below, linking the farms and properties. The railway line appeared out of an arched tunnel that bored through the middle of the mountain. The road wove between the folds of the hills.

Where the river, the railway line and the main road all met in a series of bridges was the cluster of grey rectangles and tiny cars that was Coachwood Crossing. Close by she could see the showgrounds. Now empty, it was just a huge lot with an oval show ring, neat rows of pavilions and exhibition buildings, and a rodeo arena.

The chutes were barely visible. What had she been thinking two weeks ago, when she'd agreed to make a bold anti-cruelty statement? She'd barely understood what those words meant.

Shara waited for regret to well up inside her, but it didn't. When she looked at those rodeo chutes she saw ghosts; spirits of bewildered horses waiting to be broken, and felt the same as she had two weeks ago – only more so. Wild horse racing was wrong, no matter what she had lost. It would always be wrong. And it only happened because people didn't realise. They didn't know what happened behind the scenes. They hadn't seen what she'd seen. The memory of the smell in that dairy made her inwardly gag again.

The Connemans were awful people, and even if they were put out of business, there would be more contractors supplying wild horses to rodeos. Beautiful horses, just like Goldie, would continue to be chased by teams of men, roped and forced to the ground, have their ears bitten and twisted, girths tightened around their bellies and spurred in the flanks until they bucked and bolted in terror around an arena full of laughing and jeering people. And then, off to the abattoirs with them.

A cold, wet nose touched her hand and she wrapped it around the silky fur of Hex's ears. The dog dropped to his chest with his paws out in front of him, panting and swallowing. Shara shuffled down and lay with her head in the crook between his ribs and his shoulder, arms folded across her chest, looking up at the sky, where nothing but clouds and sunshine existed.

'You okay?'

The gently spoken words made her jolt upright.

'Jess!'

Her bestie walked out onto the rock platform and sat near her, leaning back on one hand. She didn't speak, but sat, looking thoughtfully over the valley. Jess always knew when to just shut up and say nothing. Right now, she knew that no words were going to make Shara feel better. But Shara loved that Jess had climbed the highest mountain in the Coachwood Valley just to sit next to her when she felt miserable. The fact that Jess had also come on foot didn't escape her.

She closed her eyes and felt a passing cloud briefly cast a cool shadow over her face before allowing the sun to warm it again.

'Still coming tomorrow?' asked Jess.

Shara kept her eyes closed against the sunlight. 'Yep.'

She would do this ride for Goldie, his red taffy mum and his entire herd. And if she didn't have a horse, she would walk.

23

SHARA SAT SILENTLY in the back of her mother's car as they turned in through the brick gateway of the Kympania Pony Club grounds. Louise pulled up near the main arena and Shara stepped out. The seed heads of the grass grew waist-high out in the field and a warm breeze wafted lazily through long rows of open stalls, carrying with it the scent of pine shavings and seasoned timber.

Across the grounds, horses stood in the growing heat, swishing tails and stamping at flies. People brushed and saddled, buckled breastplates and tightened girths. They carried water buckets and filled hay bags.

Shara's phone buzzed. It was a message from Corey.

I found some horses we can ride, be there in ten mins.

She stood staring at the phone. He was coming. Corey was coming on the brumby ride. Mandy Conneman would never speak to him again. And he'd lose any hope of Graham ever giving Sampson back. Now what had she gone and done?

Shara looked nervously back up the main road but saw no Hilux. Should she text him back, tell him not to do it?

It's okay, I'm going to walk.

A reply buzzed straight back.

No. Wait.

She cursed quietly and checked his original message. *I found some horses* we *can ride* ... Had he already lost any hope of getting his horse back? She wondered what Mandy had told her father after their brief meeting at Corey's place.

She watched more cars drive into the grounds, recognising competitors from her mounted games days wearing jodhpurs and club uniforms; others from jump club in their long boots and velvet caps; people she'd never really met but had seen often, friends of the Blakes and the Arnolds; stockmen dressed in moleskins and checked shirts. Anita from the animal shelter arrived with several friends.

The Fairleys' rig rolled up beside her and within seconds Jess was out, backing Dodger off the loading ramp.

Shara gave her a huge hug. 'Have you heard from Luke?'

Jess shook her head. Shara could tell she was trying to be brave, so she didn't pursue the subject.

The Arnolds arrived in their enormous gooseneck truck, several horses snorting with anticipation in the back. Grace hung out the window, loud and enthusiastic, yelling hello and waving madly. In the cabin beside her, Shara could see Elliot, Rosie and Tom all squeezed in on top of each other. Another dozen horse vehicles rolled in, one after the other.

John Duggin's truck arrived and Shara's heart leapt, but she could see that John was alone. What was Corey doing? What horses had he 'found'? She tried to keep herself focused.

There was a tap on her shoulder. It was Lurlene from the RSPCA, her violent red lipstick pulled into a smile. She handed Shara several envelopes.

'These are official letters to your local government authority supporting the ban of wild horse races. One is from the RSPCA and I also managed to get some from some other animal welfare groups.' She sifted through them, showing them to Shara one by one before snapping a rubber band around them. 'Our letter also contains an information pack, outlining exactly why wild horse races are cruel, just in case they don't get it.'

Shara took the envelopes and tucked them inside her jacket. 'Thanks, Lurlene.'

Lurlene gazed around the grounds with a pleased look on her face. 'Well, you've certainly rustled up some riders.'

Shara nodded. 'It's fantastic.'

'Thought you might need help directing things,' Lurlene went on. She held out a loudspeaker and gazed lovingly at it. 'This is Larry the loudspeaker. We don't get to spend much time together these days.' She gave it an affectionate pat and passed it to Shara.

Shara was aghast. She had never ordered around a huge bunch of people before and she had certainly never barked at them through a loudhailer. 'Um, thanks. Larry'll be in good hands.'

'Now, do you have a plan? Have you mapped out the ride and thought about where you'd like people to assemble?'

'I was going to gather here in this front oval. I told the police that we'd march through town at about ten-thirty. We'll go past the rodeo grounds and along a short mountain trail for a couple of hours and then ride into town. We'll finish at the council chambers. I sent the mayor a letter telling him I wanted to present him with my petition outside the chambers at two o'clock. We've arranged to have media at each different point.'

Lurlene arched an eyebrow. 'You *are* well organised. Well, then, I'll be off.'

'Aren't you going to march?' asked Shara.

Lurlene gave a little wink. 'We have our own plans for the Connemans. We'll be seeing you soon.' And with that she was gone, striding purposefully back to her car.

Barry tapped Shara on the shoulder. 'Time to get going. I'll round everyone up, if you like.' He eyed off Larry. 'Haven't used one of those since uni.'

She shoved the loudhailer at him with relief. 'Go for it, Dad.'

Barry marched off with the speaker clamped to his mouth, calling people to attention and spouting instructions.

Shara joined Jess, Grace and Rosie and their horses on the oval.

'Sure you don't want to double?' asked Rosie. 'Buster won't mind.'

'I'll walk,' said Shara resolutely.

'Look how many people have come!' said Grace.

'There must be at least a hundred horses here,' said Jess.

The horses milled restlessly near the gate. Shara could

see the CWA crew at the clubhouse barbecue handing out bacon-and-egg rolls.

'Look! The police!' said Jess. 'Your dad's talking to them!'

'And photographers,' said Rosie, 'from the newspaper!'

Shara breathed deeply and took in the scene. Her mother was right: it was so much easier acting along-side many like-minded people. The sight of all the riders filled her with confidence and determination, and she walked up to her father and held out her hand for the loudspeaker. 'I think it's time to make my speech,' she said stiffly.

He passed it to her, smiling.

She turned on her heel, walked to the arena gates and hoisted herself up to the level of the riders. When she pushed the loudspeaker button, there was a long screech-ing sound followed by a fuzzy echo. Shara winced, waited for a spooked horse to settle, and pressed the button more firmly.

'Welcome to everyone who has come today to ride for better treatment of brumbies and to help stop wild horse races at rodeos. In the words of Mahatma Gandhi, "The greatness of a nation and its moral progress can be judged by the way its animals are treated."'

There was a spattering of claps and murmurs of approval.

'This barbaric and inhumane event takes horses from the wild and places them in an arena, where teams of men lasso them, hold them down and saddle them, then attempt to ride them. They are often roped around the neck and forcefully and brutally pulled to the ground where they are jumped on, saddled and then encouraged to buck purely for the entertainment of the crowd.

'We are not here today to stop rodeo. Most rodeos follow strict guidelines for animal welfare which they themselves have helped to develop. However, this event is not a traditional rodeo event. It is not competitive under official rodeo charters and clearly constitutes an offence under the Animal Care and Protection Act of ... ummm ... 2001.'

She saw some heads nodding. Mrs Arnold brandished her banner, nearly taking out the eye of a bystander.

'The Australian brumby is an icon. It has served and died for us in two world wars, it has worked our outback stations and helped us build a nation, yet this animal is repaid with the indignity and trauma of rodeo events like this.

'Today we are going to march to the council chambers and present the mayor with a petition, asking the council to ban all rodeos that hold this particular event. We're also going to present the petition to rodeo organisers asking them not to hold these events anymore – and not to contract stock from unethical and dodgy livestock suppliers like the Connemans.'

Shara coughed and cleared her throat. *How to end?* 'Umm, and that's all.'

There was a cheer, and the riders pushed forward towards the road – nearly a hundred of them, all bumping and jostling. All around Shara was a sea of horses' manes; greys and chestnuts and bays, all tossing and pulling with anticipation.

As she stepped down off the gate, Shara felt her father's hand take the loudspeaker. 'Well done, love.' Her dad smiled warmly at her. Beyond his proud face, a white Hilux ute rolled into the showgrounds.

Corey! She could see the shadows of two horses' heads inside the float behind, one noticeably shorter than the other. There were loud squeals, and a banging of hooves kicking at the tailgate.

'Thanks, Dad,' she said, handing him the loudhailer. She began to walk over, wondering what on earth Corey had found for her to ride. Corey stepped out of the car. He wore dark wraparound sunnies and a white shirt with the sleeves rolled halfway up his forearms. He lifted his sunnies and scanned the showgrounds. She waved.

A look of undeniable relief crossed his face and he lifted a bandaged hand to wave back as he walked out to meet her.

'What are you doing here?' she called past several other riders.

He smiled, that wickedly gorgeous smile that made her tummy twist.

'You really did come.' She wanted to throw her arms around him.

He nodded.

'You gonna unload these horses, Corey?' called John.

'In a minute,' said Corey, not taking his eyes from Shara. 'Luke lent me a horse.'

'Legsy?' Luke only had one riding horse. The only other horses he had were brumbies, young and unbroken, except for...

Corey shook his head. 'It's an absolute nightmare of a thing,' he said, his tone changing to annoyed. 'Nearly wrecked my float. Didn't stop kicking the whole way home. Tried to bite me every time I stopped and opened the door. So did your horse, so between the pair of them...'

'What horse are you talking about?' She was confused. It couldn't be the one she was thinking of.

'I don't know her name,' said Corey, turning back to the float, where the banging and clashing was getting louder. 'Luke wanted to bring her back home anyway, so he said I may as well ride her. Went on the float all right, but then she kicked the whole time. Just wouldn't stop.'

He marched ahead of her and Shara ran to catch up.

She reached out to grab him by the arm. 'Wait!'

He lifted his sunnies again and stared down at her. 'What?'

'But all Luke's horses are at ...' She searched his face to check he wasn't joking. It would be a cruel joke if he was. 'Did you drive to *Blakely Downs*?' she whispered.

He smirked.

Shara mentally tallied up the hours since she'd last spoken to him. He must have driven like the wind, with no stops, no sleeps. She looked at him questioningly.

'I knew Luke was coming back for the brumby ride, so I asked him to put some extras on the truck. He dropped them off at my place this morning.'

'*Rocko?*'

'And that white thing,' said Corey. 'He hates her. She hates him too. Between the two of them ...'

Shara turned and ran to the Hilux. She reached the long black float attached to it and clawed at the front doorhandle, squealing like an over-excited puppy. '*ROCKO!*'

A white nose and a nasty set of teeth lunged at her and she slammed the door shut again. 'Whoa! Wrong side! Sorry, Chelpie!'

She saw her father approaching the float. 'Rocko's here!' she said, running around to the other side. 'Oh my God. I thought I'd never see him again!'

She wrenched the door open and this time a chocolate

bay face looked out, ears pinned back and muzzle tight. Rocko's ears flicked forward as his eyes met Shara's.

'Hey, my beautiful boy,' she said, squeezing inside the float. Her heart all but dissolved when Rocko turned his fat quarter-horsey cheeks to her and nickered, his voice deep and old and throaty, totally familiar. She wrapped her arms around his satin-smooth neck and buried her face in his thick mane. She felt his chest rumble as he nickered again. 'I never got to say goodbye,' she whispered. 'My bestest horse in the whole world. Have you missed me?'

Then her heart stopped. Did her dad know? Was this allowed?

'Your dad said I could go and get him,' said Corey from outside the small door.

She relaxed back into Rocko's neck and exhaled.

When she pulled her head out of his mane and looked through the back of the float she could see Barry, smiling. 'Better saddle up and get riding, you still haven't earned the right to keep him.'

Without another word, Shara ripped the quick-tie knot undone. Corey dropped the tailgate, and she had Rocko saddled in minutes. She led him around to where Corey was struggling with Chelpie, trying to girth her up.

'She's a rescue mare,' Shara explained. 'She's always been sour. Luke took her from the RSPCA.'

The white mare pulled a malicious face and tried to cow-kick him. He jumped forward out of the way and lifted an elbow, blocking her bared teeth. 'She'll be okay,' said Corey.

'You'll lose Sampson for good if you come on this ride.'

He wrinkled his nose and shrugged. 'I already have, so it makes no difference now.'

Corey cut a ridiculous figure on Chelpie. His legs hung well below her belly and his big hat and wraparound sunnies just looked all wrong on the little white show pony. He held the reins in one hand, swung his legs about and sung a country-and-western tune as Chelpie let a few pigroots fly. 'Wa-hoo!' he hooted as he kicked her up.

Shara swung herself up into one of Corey's big roping saddles and sank into its couch-like seat. 'Nice,' she murmured, looking down at the pommel. She twisted around and ran a hand behind the cantle to find a big metal plate. 'Trophy saddle?'

'From the Coachwood Show,' he said.

'Ah, yes, that show,' said Shara awkwardly, trying not to remember the day Corey had watched her tumble head-over-heel off a stockyard rail.

Corey chuckled and looked away.

'Let's not go there,' said Shara, kicking Rocko up. 'Come on. Let's ride, cowboy!'

People laughed and called out to each other, bits and

spurs jingled and horses whinnied. The entire crowd surged forward.

Shara sat tall as she rode. At last she could put things right. She had her friends and her family and her community behind her, she had her good horse beneath her and she felt totally unconquerable. She patted the fat bundle of petitions that sat snug beneath her jacket, and urged Rocko onward.

24

THEY LEFT THE soft grassy oval behind, and a hundred horses' shoes clopped and clattered on the bitumen. It was an awesome noise, like the beginning of a summer rainstorm on hot corrugated iron, building into one big thundering downpour.

The road had been cleared and four empty lanes stretched ahead. Shara felt like royalty as she led the ride towards the rodeo grounds behind a single police car. Corey, Jess, Rosie and Tom rode to the left of her. Elliot clung on behind Grace on the steel grey, with his glasses half falling off, looking mildly terrified. John and Mrs Arnold were on her right. A photographer snapped away, dashing and dancing backwards in front of them. Shara rode with one hand, settling into the rhythm of Rocko's keen stride.

The road was lined with brush box trees, and beyond

them lay quiet paddocks from which cows looked up, alarmed at the commotion, and hustled their calves away. It took a good fifteen minutes to come within view of the Kympania rodeo grounds, by which time there were more photographers and a news crew standing by a white van. A cameraman hoisted a large black box to his shoulder and began shooting.

'How good is this?' said Shara. 'I can't believe how big this has turned out to be.'

But Jess's answer was not so awestruck. 'Is that what I think it is?'

The cameraman pivoted and began filming in another direction. From a side road, not a hundred metres from the rodeo grounds, a huge red semitrailer rumbled directly across in front. It slowed to a stop, blocking the entire road, and hissed as its brakes were let off. Across the cabin door, in gold swirly letters, were the words:

Bred to Buck
Conneman Brothers
Rodeo Stock Contractors

'Holy...' Shara brought Rocko to a stop and heard the rising murmur of the riders behind her. A shout went up and ricocheted back down the line. But she could feel the restless energy bustling up behind her, unwilling to slow. John rode to the front.

A cabin door swung open and Graham Conneman slid to the ground. He stood, arms folded across his chest, jaw set stubborn and hard under a broad-brimmed hat. Mark Conneman, shorter and more wiry, stepped down from the other door and walked around to join him. They stood side by side like king brown snakes, provoked, territorial and clearly angry.

Three stockmen descended from the trailer, and Mandy appeared behind them. She stepped forward and stood next to her father with hands on black-jeaned hips.

All around the sound of hoofbeats continued and the rumble of voices rose. Shara looked quickly to John.

'Just carry on riding,' he said calmly. 'They have as much right to be here as us.'

'In the middle of the road?'

He paused. 'Let's see what the police do.'

Shara was relieved to see the police car stop and two officers get out.

John urged his horse into a jog and took the lead. 'We'll go around them.'

But the truck stretched from the side road to the opposite fence and the Connemans' stockmen filled any gap. The ride was blocked. Behind Shara and her friends the procession still bustled, and she felt Rocko being nudged forward. The horses were now flank to flank, locked together in a steady push. They lifted their heads and whinnied nervously.

Shara yelled over her shoulder for the riders to back off as she tried to hold Rocko steady. He reared beneath her. She threw her arms forward to go with him, and felt the envelopes inside her jacket slip. The bundle dropped over her leg and onto the ground. 'The petitions!' Rocko spooked and leapt sideways, slamming into another horse.

Envelopes tore open under a stampede of hooves. Papers spilled out, were picked up by the breeze and carried between the horses' legs. They whirled and flapped and a current of panic shot through the horses.

Voices yelled, horses shied, papers whipped with the wind, photographers snapped. Before Shara knew it, the ride had not only come to a complete halt, but it had begun to break up, backwards, sideways, all over the place.

'No, don't give up,' yelled Shara. 'We can go around them!'

From the sidelines, Anita looked at her and shook her head.

'No...'

Anita pointed to the side street. Shara followed her gaze. Another police car rolled slowly up behind the semitrailer and three more officers got out. They were followed by an RSPCA van. A door flung open and Lurlene Spencer stepped out. From the other side came Mr Hoskins.

Graham Conneman roared, 'You've got no right to take my animals. They're my livelihood!'

'The RSPCA are seizing the brumbies,' said Shara, spinning around and facing Corey, who was holding a prancing Chelpie steady, pulling at the bit as she drummed her hooves on the bitumen.

'Yyyup! They're seizing all the Connemans' animals.'

'Sampson?'

'Hope so!'

Shara felt a rush of hope that in some way she might have helped him get ownership of his good horse. 'Oh my God, this will shut down the whole rodeo! The Connemans are supplying all the cattle, too.'

Mandy shot Corey a look of fury. 'You'll never ride in rodeo again, Corey Duggin.' She pointed at him. 'We'll black-ban you! We'll rig it so you never get good stock again. You'll pull the most feral cattle and get the worst draws. No one will sponsor you because they'll know you'll only ever lose! No one will even speak to you after this!'

'This isn't about you, Mandy,' said Corey.

'No,' she replied. 'It was never about me, obviously.'

Corey held her gaze for a short moment before riding Chelpie towards the Connemans' stockmen. Shara watched him roll his spurs up Chelpie's ribs, and the dainty white horse swished her tail angrily and bit at the air in front of her. 'Follow me!' he said, waving Shara after him.

'What about all the papers?' she called back. Rocko cantered on the spot and she felt the skin tighten over his wither as he bunched his muscles beneath her.

'Leave them, we don't need them!' Chelpie bounced sideways, clearing a big space, and Corey sent her leaping forward. She rushed at the people blocking her, teeth bared. They scattered.

'Good girl, Chelpie!' said Shara.

'She's a weapon on legs,' said Corey.

Behind them, the other riders filtered through the small gap between the truck and the fence, looking down at the Conneman staff as they clattered past. In a huge nodding and tossing and tail-swishing throng, with clanging stirrups and brushing saddles, they began to move slowly past the rodeo grounds.

The front fence looked as though it had just had a lick of fresh paint to spruce it up for the event. Shara could smell cut grass and knew volunteers would have spent long days getting the grounds ready. In the gateway, an elderly couple sat under a beach brolly with a pouch of small change on their laps, an esky between them like a coffee table. Their faces were stony as their eyes followed the procession.

People in fluoro vests directed a dozen or so cars into a neat row beside the arena. It was a poor turnout. People must have heard about the brumby ride.

But the show went on. Crooning cattle and a loud voice broadcast over the event, cutting through the din of the brumby ride. Guitars twanged and horses whinnied. As the thunderous noise of horses' hooves neared, the people in the grounds began walking to the roadside, staring at the huge procession coming their way.

They waited with hard faces, watching. One threw a Coke can out onto the road. Shara felt a hot thwack on her cheek and something bounced off her shoulder. A hot chip? 'They're throwing food at me!'

'Just keep going,' said John beside her. 'Don't react.'

The whole cardboard cup came next, complete with tomato sauce, and she dodged the spray of greasy crumbs and red goo. Rocko stepped sideways as the cup tumbled down his shoulder. 'And they say brumbies are feral,' said Shara, as she looked down at the red splatters on her shirt.

'Hey!' Corey yelled angrily.

'It's all right. I'm fine,' said Shara quickly. 'It was just some sauce. It was nothing.'

'Hey, it's Corey,' yelled someone.

'Yeah, it is, and that's my *friend* you're chucking stuff at,' he yelled back.

'Don't get in a fight, Corey,' Shara pleaded. This was the last thing she needed.

'Look straight ahead and keep riding.' John trotted up beside his son. 'Don't bite, Corey. You knew it would be like this.'

Corey looked away, holding Chelpie in a steady jog-trot, his feet jammed down hard in his stirrups. Chelpie, as though feeding on the hostility that percolated around her, pressed her ears to the back of her head and screwed her nostrils into the nastiest face Shara had ever seen on a horse. She pulled her lips back, bit at the air in front of her and rolled her eyes towards the crowd.

'I like your little show pony, Duggin!' another voice teased.

Corey spun Chelpie's hindquarters towards the voice and rolled a spur up her side. Chelpie lashed out with both back legs.

Laughter rippled through the rodeo crowd.

'Corey!' John warned.

Corey lowered his spurs, but Chelpie still swished her tail and the rodeo crowd stepped back as he pranced past, despite the timber fence rails.

'You okay?' asked Shara.

'Just gotta get past this crowd.' He shot her a sideways

grin. 'I like this horse, though. She's got some attitude.'

'She's done heaps of dressage.'

Corey gathered up Chelpie's reins and pushed his seat into her, making the mare spring into a bouncy passage. She arched her neck, fanned her tail from side to side and lifted her knees one at a time in big, exaggerated movements. Corey lifted his cowboy hat and waved it to the rodeo crowd in a grand, sweeping gesture. Before he could clamp the hat back on his head, Chelpie pigrooted and bumped him out of the saddle for a stride.

More chuckles wove through the onlookers. Corey sent the little white horse in an extended trot along the fenceline, legs punching and toes flicking dramatically out in front.

'Show-off,' John muttered beside Shara.

She rolled her eyes and watched Corey finish his dressage workout with a half-circle to change direction, then a collected trot straight back to the rodeo people. He halted, gathered his reins in one hand, saluted in true dressage style and then dropped Chelpie's reins.

'I give you a fifty-two for that, Corey!' a woman called.

'You big girl! Get some jodhpurs!' yelled another.

Corey rode towards a small crowd that he seemed to know. But as he neared them, more riders pushed their horses menacingly towards him and Shara was glad of the fence between them.

'We're not riding against rodeo,' he told them. 'We're riding against the wild horse race. It's crap. It's not even a recognised event. It's giving rodeo a bad name.'

'Yeah, well, your ride has gone and halted the whole event,' said a man in a red shirt. 'We travelled for miles to get here and now the whole thing's cancelled. People have been working for months to run this event.'

'It's not our fault the event was cancelled,' argued Corey. 'It was the dodgy stock contractors.'

'Those dodgy contractors have been supplying you with good horses to ride for the last couple of years, mate. You're a hypocrite.' The red-shirted man walked away.

'Oh, come on, Danny,' Corey implored.

'All the stock's being seized,' said another. 'They're perfectly healthy, nothing wrong with them.'

Behind them Shara saw a stock truck – the one from the animal shelter? – drive into the grounds and head towards the yards. Jess gasped behind her. 'They're taking the brumbies!'

A cheer went through the protest riders and horses began shifting restlessly, eager to move.

Corey slipped off his horse and handed the reins to Shara. She inwardly groaned as she took them. 'Don't go in there, Corey, you'll get killed!'

'They're my mates,' he said. He slipped through the fence and ran after them.

Next to Shara, John cursed quietly. He reined his horse about and kept moving with the brumby ride. 'Keep riding, Shara.'

Corey looked back over his shoulder as he ran into the rodeo grounds. 'Wait for me, Sharsy!'

'Easy, Rocko.' Shara tried to hold her horse steady but it was like being caught in a rip. A hundred horses were moving away from her and she could hardly hold Rocko and Chelpie against the undercurrent. Jess, Grace and Rosie were well out of sight, at the front of the ride.

Rocko and Chelpie shifted about and she struggled to hold them off each other. Rocko bounced beneath her and Chelpie swung her hindquarters, tossing her mane and gnashing her teeth.

Shara saw John's back disappearing in the sea of riders and looked back into the showgrounds at Corey, who had reached his friends and stood arguing with them between the parked cars. His arms were waving around as he talked. The men were leaning forward and yelling back. They didn't look in agreement at all.

As she looked back up the line of brumby riders and wondered whether to wait for Corey or to just keep riding, Lawson Blake rode up behind her on a small brown horse. 'Look out,' he said. 'Here comes trouble.'

He nodded towards the stockyards. Graham Conneman, his fists clenched, was marching towards the car park.

Shara reined Rocko away. 'I can't watch.'

But a hand grabbed hers. Lawson was off his horse, wrapping his reins over her arm. 'Hold Chocky a minute.'

'I can't hold all of them,' she complained, as Chelpie lunged and the gelding pulled away. 'Chelpie's a psycho!'

Lawson shut her up with a look. 'Corey's out there, sticking his neck out for you. You do the right thing and wait for him.' And with one hand on the fence rail and two feet leaping over it he was off, after Corey.

Shara had so much trouble trying to keep the horses together, she couldn't watch anyway.

She did see the last of the brumby riders disappear up the road without her, and she listened to the sound of their hooves fading. Her parents were going to freak if she didn't show up at the sausage sizzle.

Finally, she managed to get Chelpie's reins tied around the branch of a tree, and Lawson's gelding tied well away from her, so she could watch what was happening. In the middle of the car park, a crowd of people had gathered. Through them, she caught a glimpse of Corey's friends restraining him by the elbows as he struggled and yelled at Graham, who in turn was held back by Lawson. Two police officers walked briskly towards the scene, waving people away.

Corey stopped struggling when he saw them. But Graham only yelled louder and the police had to help

Lawson restrain him. The crowd moved in closer and obscured Shara's view, and she rode up and down the road trying to see what was happening. Through a gap in the mob, she saw a pair of denim-clad legs writhing on the ground beneath two police officers, and she prayed they weren't Corey's.

And then Lawson broke from the crowd, dragging Corey by the shirt sleeve. He had lost his hat, and Lawson pulled him along so fast he struggled to keep his feet. Corey took a last glance back at the rodeo grounds and Shara saw the red-shirted man dip his hat to him. Corey lifted a hand, turned towards Shara and sprinted in her direction.

25

COREY RODE IN SILENCE, letting the rhythmic nod of Chelpie's walk pull the reins back and forth in his hands, in time with her stride. He turned and looked back at the rodeo every twenty metres or so. Lawson cantered ahead.

'If they're real friends, you'll see them again,' said Shara quietly.

Corey didn't answer.

'Besides,' she said, trying to sound cheerful. 'You could have a real future in dressage.'

'No, thanks,' he said, sounding flat. He picked up his reins and kicked Chelpie into a canter. 'Let's catch up with the ride.'

Shara followed for several minutes, enjoying the canter and the movement of air it brought to her face until they reached the tail end of the ride. The horses, perspiring now from the excitement and contagious energy of each other, walked along the road with barely a breath of wind to clear the swelling dust or to dry their sweat-soaked coats.

They reached a long, grassy stretch that followed a powerline up and over the mountain. It was steep, but wide enough that riders could travel alongside each other, talking and laughing and enjoying the day. Kids scooted back and forth on their ponies, and parents nagged them to behave. Dogs trotted happily alongside, tongues flapping from their mouths.

At the top, Shara and Corey stood their horses side by side, letting a gentle breeze cool their skin. Chelpie blew heavily from the effort of carrying Corey and he jumped off and loosened her girth. 'Better lead her for a while,' he said flatly. 'Don't want her blowing a gasket.'

Shara slipped off Rocko and did the same. They stood aside and let the riders pass onto a pebbly fire trail leading to a large forest reserve.

A sudden piercing whistle shot through her ears. Corey turned to look behind them, and curled a thumb and a forefinger beneath his teeth. 'Danny!' He waved like an excited schoolkid. 'Emma!' Down the track, Shara recognised the man in the red shirt, Corey's friend. A woman rode beside him, and trailing behind them on lead ropes were two small kids on adult-sized horses, barely big enough to stay in the saddle. They held tight to the horns of big western saddles with their feet in little

216

stirrup clogs. Their round white helmets on their tiny twiggy bodies reminded Shara of Chupa Chups lollipops.

'The kids talked us into it,' said Danny as he rode closer. 'They started crying when they saw the brumbies being put through the yards.'

'Jackson said the stockmen were mean,' said Emma.

'He's a smart kid,' said Corey. 'You guys should listen to him.'

Emma held his hat out. 'I told him that event was a disgrace.' She looked at Shara. 'Did you organise this ride?' She legged her horse over, leaned across and held out a hand. 'I'm Emma. Good on ya, matey.'

'Some of the others are coming too,' said Danny. 'Nothing else to do, now that the rodeo's over.' He still looked unimpressed. Then he ran his eyes over Chelpie. 'Where the *hell* did you get that horse? You should put it through the chutes. I reckon it'd buck like a demon.'

Corey shot him a *shut-up* look and then rolled his eyes at Shara.

Danny quickly shut up. 'Oh. Sorry.'

'She'd ditch both you idiots,' said Emma.

'I wanna run, Dad,' said one of the kids, waving a whip at the flank of his horse. 'Make him run again!'

'Me too!' demanded the other, pulling and yanking on the pommel of the saddle.

'Better do as I'm told,' said Danny with a wave.

'There's a free sausage sizzle at the top,' Corey called after him.

As Shara watched them trot away in a little mob, she thought how glad she was that she hadn't cancelled.

She looked back down the line and watched all the horses coming up the trail. They were an awesome sight as they clambered, pushing their shoulders into the climb; a wonderful mix of all horsey types, with their varying styles of leather and buckles and their different dress codes. Whether stockmen, dressage riders, pony-clubbers or weekend trail riders, the riders were all one and the same, all horse lovers who cared about the wellbeing and dignity of their horses' wild cousins.

This was just a wonderful thing to be a part of. Her dad had been right. This wasn't about her. This was all about Goldie and his mother and horses just like them.

Looking back over the view, Shara could see across the golden-green fields, the grey snake of bitumen cutting through them, lined with gum trees and alive with traffic. The Connemans' big red semi was still parked across the road and police cars and other vehicles were dotted around it. Tiny people walked between them. The rodeo grounds were emptying fast, with catering vans driving away and tents being dismantled.

The yards were still full of cattle, and among them, a mob of horses stood quietly in the sun, mostly browns and chestnuts, swishing tails at flies and nuzzling into each other for comfort: the brumbies, the wild horses. They would be spared. Nearby was the animal rescue truck. She wondered where the brumbies would end up. Somewhere much better than a wild horse race, she hoped.

'Sorry we shut down the rodeo,' Shara said to Corey.

'They're good people,' he said. 'None of them want to hurt horses.'

'I guess every horse sport has its good people and bad people.'

'They sure do,' said Corey. 'Now, did you say there'll be a sausage sizzle? I'm starving.'

'Half an hour down the fire trail,' she said. 'But it's not free. Grace is going to kill you for saying that! She wanted to raise money for brumby groups.'

'Whoops.' Then Corey patted his pockets. 'Hope I get a freebie. I've got no cash on me.'

'I'll shout you one, come on.' Shara led Rocko back onto the trail and walked along, finding a space where she and Corey could be together alone.

'Now do you believe me?' he said, as he led Chelpie along beside her.

'Believe what?'

'That I like you.'

'Yes.' She held out her hand and he wrapped a strong, calloused hand around hers, entwining their fingers

219

together. She bumped her shoulder to his and they walked the fire trail together, leading Chelpie and Rocko behind them on long loopy reins.

The smell of frying onions and sizzling sausages hit them before they got to the reserve. 'I could eat about ten of those,' said Corey, tethering Chelpie to a tree.

Grace stood nearby with a bum-bag, collecting coins and handing out tickets. A hotplate sizzled, and Chan bundled slices of white bread into serviettes, ready to be made up into sangers.

The CWA women had also set up a stall with trays of home-baked treats: cherry and coconut slice, lamingtons, hedgehogs, honey joys and chocolate crackles.

'Now, that's what I call real food,' Jess was saying with approval. 'None of that industrial processed rubbish. Real food made with real ingredients. I want one of everything!' She piled cakes onto a small paper plate, oblivious to Chan glaring at her.

More cars parked nearby and a horse truck drove in behind them. 'Hey, Jess,' said Shara. 'Is that Luke?'

Jess looked up. 'Huh?'

Shara pointed to the truck, which had Ryan Blake at the wheel and a wild-haired boy in the passenger seat.

Jess spilled her cakes everywhere. A kelpie darted in and began devouring them from the ground. 'Luke.' She looked wide-eyed at Shara. 'I'm not allowed to talk to him... for five weeks, four days and twelve hours.'

'But who's counting?' said Shara. 'Your parents aren't here. Go and hug him!'

Jess jumped over the kelpie and ran to the truck. Luke leapt out and took her in a big swinging hug, lifting her feet up off the ground and whirling her in big circles. Shara sighed. They were so cute together.

She picked up a stack of sausage sangers, all dripping with onion juice and tomato sauce, handed three to Corey and gave him a wink. 'I got friends in high places too, you know.' She took one more for herself and sank her teeth into it.

They made their way to Ryan's truck, munching on the sausages as they walked.

'Thanks for the lend of the horse,' Corey said to Luke. 'She travel okay?'

'Nup.'

'Did you bring Legsy?' asked Shara.

'Nup,' said Luke. He walked around to the back, where Ryan was winching the tailgate down. 'I was already out at Blakely Downs when I heard about the brumby ride. Rusty and Tinks were in the home paddock, and I thought they'd be perfect to bring along – they were victims of a wild horse race.' He shrugged. 'So I came back.'

Shara gasped with delight. 'You're a genius!'

Ryan led a rusty-coloured yearling and a small brown foal, about six months old, down the loading ramp. Their coats were sun-bleached and shaggy, but they were in fine body condition.

Luke took Rusty's rope from Ryan and tied him to the side of the truck. 'These guys were heli-mustered up north for a wild horse race – both their parents died in the muster. Tinks' mum died giving birth after being galloped for hours in forty-five-degree heat. The stallion never even made it to the yards.'

Shara noticed a journalist, with a camera slung around his neck, watching them and listening. He walked over. 'Any chance of an interview?' he asked Luke.

Shara saw her parents stepping out of the four-wheel drive in the car park. She ran over to them. 'Luke brought his brumbies along,' she said, bursting with happiness and excitement. 'They're doing a story on him. Some of Corey's friends abandoned the rodeo and rode with us instead. The Connemans have been arrested. It's been such an *amazing* day!' She was talking a million miles an hour, but she couldn't help it. She threw her arms around her dad's neck.

'Don't forget your appointment with the mayor,' Barry whispered in her ear. 'Two o'clock.'

26

AS THEY GIRTHED UP for the second leg of the ride, Lurlene Spencer approached Shara with a bundle of papers tucked under her arm. 'I managed to scrape a lot of them off the road,' she said, handing the tattered papers to Shara. She had bound them with a piece of hay band knotted in the middle. 'The girls at the office reprinted some of the formal paperwork. It should still do the job. But please don't drop it this time.'

'I promise I won't,' said Shara, as she lifted a foot into her stirrup.

The ride continued down a gentle slope over the other side of the mountain, the horses quiet-footed on the decomposing leaves of eucalypt forest. The voices of the riders murmuring over the hoofbeats sounded weary. Shara noticed the silence of the forest. The currawongs and finches had fled as more than a hundred horses marched sombrely through. Every so often there was a sudden *crash, crash* of a wallaby bolting unseen through the thick underscrub, cracking branches and crunching leaves.

Shara rode in silence, thinking of Goldie. She tried to picture him in his new home. A family, John had said. Was it a girl, she wondered, who would watch him fill out into a muscular young horse? Or was it a guy who would break and train him at home? Would Goldie go on to compete in rodeo? She had been too shocked to ask, but she would ask John when she got the chance. Maybe the people might even send her a photo of him now and then, looking loved and well cared for. That would be nice, she decided.

She sighed and continued down the trail, which soon came back to the bitumen road but at a point closer to the town of Kympania. It was a small town, unremarkable except for its beautiful council chambers surrounded by huge old fig trees sprawling their massive grey roots over the lawns.

Most riders continued through the main street and made their way back towards the rodeo grounds, while Shara and her friends presented the petitions.

The mayor was a mayoress. She welcomed Shara and her friends and listened politely while Shara explained their cause. Then she gave an unconvincing smile while posing during the handing-over of the petition for the photographer, who took one shot and raced off to his next job. The mayor also raced off to her next job, leaving Shara, Jess, Grace, Rosie, Tom, Luke and Corey to show themselves out.

Shara watched her disappear with brisk steps through the large open doors of the council chambers, carrying the bundle of papers. 'I hope she finds time to read them,' she said out loud.

As they rode out of town, Shara and Corey let the others ride ahead. They passed the rodeo grounds and the Connemans' truck, which had been moved to the side of the road. She was relieved to see no sign of them. All that was left of the ride was a sea of trampled horse poo along the bitumen.

'It'll wash away in the next rain,' shrugged Corey.

'No different to a cattle drive,' said Shara, looking up ahead to the showgrounds, where rest and a cool drink waited for her.

Behind his Hilux ute, Corey tethered Chelpie to the float and pulled off her saddle. On the other side, Shara pulled the big roping saddle off Rocko. They appeared at the back of the ute at the same time, and in perfect unison, flipped their fenders over the seats of their saddles and draped the breastplates on top. Then they both tossed everything effortlessly into the back.

'Oh *no*,' Shara said suddenly.

'What now?' said Corey, looking around in alarm.

She took him by the shirt and dragged him to the side of the float. He looked at her, puzzled.

She lowered her voice to a whisper. 'I think there's a security guard coming.'

'Uh-oh,' he said.

She looked up at his eyes, heavy-lidded and weary but still twinkling with amusement. A faint tinge of bruising still rimmed his cheekbone. She reached up, took his hat off and put it on her own head.

He ran a hand through his shaggy hat hair and took a step closer to her. 'What'll we *do*?'

'It's okay. I'll cover your arse,' she said, sliding her hands around his waist and down into the back pockets of his jeans. 'Just follow my lead.'

He leaned down and ran his lips, softly, barely there, along her neck and under her ear. 'Like this?' She felt his leg wrap around hers as he stared down at her, meeting her gaze.

'No, like this.' Shara leaned up towards him. As she kissed his lips, she felt his hand run up the back of her neck and pull her closer. His kiss was strong and gentle and very... very... long. By the time he let go of her she felt she'd been turned inside-out. Her breath came in short rasps and her legs were wobbly.

'Is he gone yet?' Corey whispered, nuzzling her ear.

'Who?'

'The security dude.'

'Oh, him. No, I think he's getting closer.' She kissed him again and pulled his hat brim down low to block out the universe.

27

THE GIRLS CLUSTERED AROUND Shara's kitchen bench, eagerly reading the morning news.

'Look how much coverage we got,' said Shara. 'Two articles in one paper.'

KYMPANIA WILD HORSE RACE AXED

ORGANISERS of the Kympania Rodeo have cancelled all future wild horse races following pressure from animal welfare groups.

The decision was prompted by protests at the rodeo and also by the threat of legal action from the RSPCA.

The RSPCA last night confirmed the organisation was opposed to the event. 'A carnival environment is far removed from any animal's natural habitat. When you compound this problem with neglect and cruelty, an animal's life becomes extremely miserable.'

The Conneman brothers, who supply horses for the event, said, 'The event is not cruel. The horses love every minute of it.'

A rodeo association spokesperson said it followed strict guidelines for animal welfare and it did not wish to breach them in any way. 'The wild horse race is not a traditional rodeo event. It is not a competitive event, but purely for entertainment.'

|||||||||||||||||||||||||||||||||||||||||||||||||||||||||||||||||||||||||||||||||||||||||||||||||||||||

BRUMBIES SEIZED; CONTRACTOR CHARGED

Police and RSPCA officers seized horses and cattle from stock contractors at the Kympania rodeo, citing animal neglect and cruelty.

Graham and Mark Conneman were charged with breach of duty of care and failing to provide adequate veterinary treatment after brumbies in their care were found sick and dying at a remote property.

Mark Conneman had prior convictions of animal neglect.

'And don't forget the magazine article with Luke, Tinks and Rusty,' said Jess. 'That will come out next month.'

Barry kicked off his boots in the doorway and joined them. 'How do you like your new-found fame, girls?'

'Did you see the paper, Dad?'

'Better results when you go about things properly, hey?'

'It's fantastic,' said Shara. 'Did you read these articles?'

'I did, and I'm proud of you,' said Barry.

'I hope they never get the horses back. Lurlene said that a lot of the time courts give them their animals back because they need them to make a living.'

'Well, we'll just have to wait and see,' said Barry. 'But you have done those horses a really big favour already. I'm sure everything will work out for them.'

'I hope so,' said Shara. Again, she couldn't help thinking of Goldie.

The driveway down to John's surgery was long, straight and lined on either side with tall white flooded gums. The early morning light shone through them in soft golden streaks. In the small paddocks behind the trees, the bandaged horses and baby calves munched on their feed.

Shara rode Rocko towards the house.

'Hey,' said a drowsy voice.

'Hey.'

In the open doorway was Corey, brown hair every-where, yawning and tucking in his T-shirt. He jumped off the front verandah and waved her to the stables. 'Come and see the horses that were seized from the Connemans.'

Shara tied Rocko to a hitching rail. She peered into the first stable and instantly recognised the red taffy mare. 'Goldie's mum.' The mare had the same softness in her eyes that had been in the little colt's. When Shara stepped near her, however, the softness vanished and her eyes became wily and fearful. She lifted her head and backed away.

'I'm going to buy her. She's had a horrible life, poor thing,' said Corey.

'She's very pretty,' said Shara. 'What are you going to do with her?'

'Put her out to stud. Lawson Blake said I could put Biyanga over her.'

'You might get a silver taffy,' said Shara. Biyanga was jet black. 'It would be just like Goldie, only not so naughty.' She thought of all Goldie's antics: Mr Hickling's lychee trees and Mrs Jenkins's washing.

She felt Corey's arm slip over her shoulder. 'You can have her next foal. It can be your birthday pressie.'

She put her hand on his arm and looked up at him.

'How did you know it was my birthday today?'

'Jess drilled me. You'll have to wait a while, though, till she's healthier and all that sort of thing. And until I suck up to your dad a bit.'

She smiled. 'He's a lot cooler than he was a week ago.' Then she looked at the mare again. It would be so nice to have another little Goldie. A hardy mountain brumby crossed with Biyanga's bloodlines. 'Do you mean it?' she asked. 'I could really have a foal from her?'

'Only if you promise not to run off with any other cowboys. I know what a groupie you are.'

She whacked him. 'I'm *so* not into cowboys.'

'Yes you are, you *love* them,' he said, picking her up and lifting her in the air. She put her arms around his neck.

'I've got something for you now,' he said, putting her down and reaching into the pocket of his jeans. He fumbled around for a while and pulled out a small black velvet pouch with a gold tie-string.

'What is it?' She untied the string and shook the bag over her palm. 'My horsey charm!'

'It was stuck in my shirt. I found it when I was shoving my clothes in the wash.'

'Ohhhh, my horsey,' she said. 'It's meant to be Rocko.' She kissed it and then reached up and kissed him, so happy to have it back. 'Thank you.'

'Keep tipping, there's another one in there too.'

Shara opened the tie-strings wide and peered in. 'Oh wow.' She poked a finger in and fished out another tiny horse charm; gold with a silver mane. 'It's a little taffy!' She put a hand to Corey's face. 'Did they surrender Sampson?'

'Nah. Graham will just transfer his papers to Mandy. She's always wanted him.'

Shara pulled a face.

'At least he'll be better looked after with her,' said Corey with a shrug. 'She cares a lot more about her horses than her dad does.'

The sound of tyres on gravel rumbled behind them and Shara looked out of the stable block. Lawson's truck rolled down the driveway with three people in the front. 'Jessy and Luke!' she said happily.

'Thank God, they can take this woeful white mare back to where she came from. She's upsetting all the other horses. I don't know what it is about her.'

'Chelpie's a wild white water demon,' said Shara. 'That's what Jess reckons.' She skipped out to the driveway. Two velvety muzzles poked out of the truck's side windows. She jumped up and gave them a rub. 'Hey, little cuties!'

Jess stuck her head out the window. 'Happy birthday, best bestie!'

'Thanks! I thought you were grounded!'

'I've been officially pardoned. What did you get?'

Shara jumped off the side of the truck. 'Look what Corey gave me!'

Lawson Blake got out, slammed the door and walked to the back of the truck to begin winching down the tailgate.

John Duggin came out of the surgery, his phone clamped to the side of his head. 'Yep. Yep. Whereabouts? How many? Uh-huh. Jesus. Hmmm, maybe. Okay then, Lurlene.' He hung up and shook his head with disapproval.

'The Connemans have another mob of wildies somewhere down in New South Wales,' he said. 'They haven't paid the brumby runner and now there are six horses headed for the slaughterhouse.'

'Where in New South Wales?' asked Lawson.

'On the tablelands, not far over the border,' John said. 'A place called Mathew's Flat.'

Shara noticed Jess glance anxiously at Luke.

Luke looked as though he'd just been punched.

'They're looking for someone with a spare truck, some good-quality yards and a kind heart.'

'Well, that cuts Lawson out,' mumbled Jess.

Luke and Lawson exchanged glances. Something ran through the exchange that Shara couldn't quite pick up on, but she could tell that this was about more than just the brumbies. Jess suddenly looked intensely worried too. Shara decided to shut up and keep out of it.

'Might be time to go back, Luke,' said Lawson, in a voice that was uncharacteristically gentle.

Luke's jaw was set tight. He nodded. 'You coming too?'

'Yeah, mate,' said Lawson. He switched his attention back to John. 'Tell Lurlene we'll drop these horses out at Blakely Downs and then head straight to New South Wales. I'll ring her up and get the details in a couple of days.'

Chelpie was loaded in a matter of minutes and Jess hung off the side of the truck door hugging Luke through the window as it rolled back out the driveway. She jumped off at the letterbox and stood watching the truck disappear up the road.

'What was that all about?' Shara asked her when she came back down the driveway.

'Luke's father lives down there in Mathew's Flat. He hasn't seen him since he was four years old. It's where his mother died.'

'How did she die?' asked Shara. Luke was always so closed and mysterious.

Jess shook her head. 'I don't know. He doesn't talk about it. He never talks about his past.'

'Oh.'

'I'm going to walk home,' said Jess. She looked miserable again, as she always was when Luke went away.

Shara was beginning to know how she felt. She looked at her watch. Her parents were taking her back to Canningdale straight after lunch. 'Just one minute while I say goodbye to Corey and I'll double you home,' she said to Jess.

The goodbye kiss took longer than Shara anticipated – she just couldn't let go of Corey. *Just one minute* turned into about another ten, until Jess started coughing exaggeratedly outside the door of the stable.

Corey slung his arm over Shara's shoulder. 'I'll come down on a weekend and visit you. Me and Jess and Luke, we'll all come down.'

He gave her a leg-up onto Rocko and walked beside her as she rode out of the building.

Jess vaulted up behind her and as Shara leaned down to give Corey one last kiss, Jess kicked Rocko in the flanks. 'That's enough, let's get going before you both make me puke.'

'You can talk!' said Shara indignantly, as Rocko broke into a trot. 'Bye!' she called back to Corey.

He stood in the big open doorway of the old wooden stables and smiled his gorgeous smile, a smile she knew she'd dream about constantly until she saw him again.

28

SHARA SAT IN THE back of the car with her phone in her hand, flicking messages back and forth with her friends. It was early evening and the sky was darkening already. Barry brought the car down a gear. Up ahead were the old red-brick buildings of Canningdale College, with their creamy archways and timber window frames, surrounded by a small farm.

Barry flicked on the indicator and crossed hand-over-hand, bringing the car and float carefully through the gates. They drove past the dorms, the Animal Science labs and the Agricultural Technologies building to the stables and horse paddocks.

Rocko whinnied loudly in the back of the float, and out in the paddocks a horse answered with a high-pitched whicker that reminded Shara of Goldie. But then, everything reminded her of Goldie right now.

Barry stopped the car by the gate to the horse paddock.

'Keep going to the stables, Dad,' she said. 'We can unload Rocko there. I have to get him an extra rug, it's freezing down here.'

'This is a good spot,' Barry insisted.

'Whatever.' The last thing she needed now was an argument with her dad. She stepped out of the car, pausing a moment to stretch her travel-cramped legs. An icy wind made its way into her lungs, bringing with it the smell of the piggery. She took a moment to take in the country. A cool gust grabbed at her shirt, lifting and flapping it.

On the float behind, Rocko pawed impatiently. As if in response, there was another whicker in the distance.

Shara looked out across the paddock to where a new horse walked towards them. 'Oh, look, it's a silver taffy! Gosh, they all sound the same.'

Barry laughed.

She looked closer. The horse walked to a bucket and picked it up in its teeth, then tossed it up and down before throwing it halfway across the paddock. 'Oh my God, it's *Goldie*,' she squealed. She looked at her dad, confused. 'Are the new owners keeping him here?'

She didn't know whether to be overjoyed or horrified. It would be absolute torture watching someone else enjoying Goldie. Her mind raced. How would any of the kids from Canningdale have heard about him? She hadn't been in touch with any of her classmates all holidays, not even Stacey. 'Did one of the students buy him?'

'Yes,' smiled Barry. 'A really nice girl, from a really nice family, just like John said.'

'Who?'

Her dad chuckled.

'*Who*, Dad? Why are you smiling like that?'

'I'm proud of you, Shara. You really did put things right, with dignity and selflessness.'

'He's...?' Shara didn't dare say it. She'd been crushed once before.

'He's yours, love,' said Barry. 'Goldie is yours. He's gone to the very best of homes.'

'Oh, Dad!' Shara threw her arms around his neck. 'You knew! You knew the whole time, and you let me *suffer*.'

He squeezed her, still chuckling. 'Stop snivelling on me now,' he said. 'Go out and say hello to your new horse.' He reached into the boot and handed her something lumpy wrapped in stripy paper. 'Happy birthday.'

It was a silver halter, cob size. 'Perfect for a horse called Goldie!' Shara exclaimed happily. She gave her dad another quick hug and then slipped through the fence.

Goldie rolled the bucket along with his nose as she walked towards him. Suddenly he looked up and saw her, stopped what he was doing and pricked his ears. Then he flung his thick, silvery mane about in exaggerated, happy nods.

'Hey there, stranger, did you miss me?'

Goldie nodded again, nickered softly and broke into a trot. He reached her and nudged his sweet golden face into her hip. She ran her hands along his cheeks, closed her eyes and rested her face on his forehead. 'No more rodeos,' she whispered softly. 'And we can even go and visit your mum in the holidays.'

She felt a pull at her shoulder and, before she knew it, Goldie had hold of the new halter in his teeth and was trotting away from her, his tail in the air.

'Hey!' she yelled, running after him. 'Give that back!'

The colt broke into a canter. Rocko galloped after him from the gateway, where Barry had been holding him, and the two horses scooted around the paddock, bucking and kicking. Goldie waved the halter teasingly around in his teeth.

She walked back to the gate and let herself through. 'Sorry about the halter, Baz.'

Her dad looked tolerant.

'I'll find it in the morning.' Shara stood, shoulder to shoulder with her dad, watching her two horses canter down and up a small gully, wheel about at the fence and gallop back again. She put her elbows and chin on the fence rail and her father did the same, and together they watched the pink and gold of the sky sink behind the boree trees and felt the chill on the wind of the approaching winter. The shapes of the horses grew darker until their silhouettes grazed peacefully beside each other.

Shara finally turned and took her bags from the car. She could smell shepherd's pie baking in the big school ovens. They would be dishing it up any minute, with soggy, grey-green broccoli and watery carrots. Jess would have sent her at least half a dozen emails by now, and she couldn't wait to tell Corey about her new horse. As though on cue, her phone buzzed.

> Bring him home next hols and I'll help you
> start him. Bags first sit. He'll buck like a pro.

Corey already knew! Unbelievable! She thumbed a message back.

> I don't do rodeo. And nor does my horse!

Acknowledgements

SPECIAL THANKS to my beautiful girls, Annabelle and Ruby, for being so good and patient while Mum's been locked away working, to Anthony for your endless love and support, and to my mum for looking after my little wildies so I could write.

Thanks to Katherine Waddington of the Australian Brumby Alliance for your encouragement, stories, photos, experiences and knowledge about wild horses; to Kath Massey of the Hunter Valley Brumby Association, and to Christine O'Rourke from Guy Fawkes Heritage Horse Association for showing me your beautiful Guy Fawkes horses.

Not nearly enough credit is given to editors, designers, marketing teams and publishing pros in the success of a book. It takes so many more people than just a lone author. So, to the entire team at Allen & Unwin, whose skills and talent have made my books come to life, my heartfelt thanks. And another extra-special thanks to my publisher, Sarah Brenan, and my editor, Hilary Reynolds; I learn so much more every time I work with you.

About the Author

KAREN WOOD has been involved with horses for most of her life. Her most special horse is a little chestnut stockhorse called Reo. Karen is married with two children and lives on the Central Coast, New South Wales.

www.diamondspirit.net

DIAMOND
SPIRIT

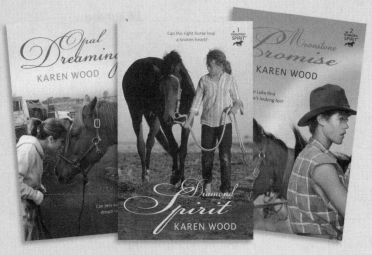

Have you read the first three books in the Diamond Spirit series?

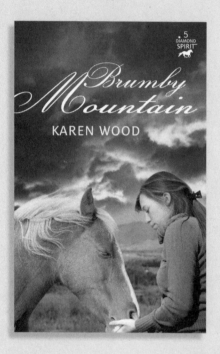

BRUMBY MOUNTAIN

In the fifth book of the Diamond Spirit series,
can Jess, Luke and their friends foil the brumby
runners and save the wild mountain horses from
their cruel fate? And in going back to Matty's Flat,
will Luke discover where he really belongs?